Angelina's Journey

Other books by Gwen Beaudean Thoma, EdD

Two children's books
No More Biting
The Cat Named Bud
Three murder mysteries
Living with Murder for Thirty Years
Whatever Happened to Sara
The King of Hearts

Angelina's Journey

Gwen Beaudean Thoma, EdD

Copyright © 2020 by Gwen Beaudean Thoma, EdD.

Library of Congress Control Number:		2020913343
ISBN:	Hardcover	978-1-6641-1913-0
	Softcover	978-1-6641-1939-0
	eBook	978-1-6641-1912-3

All rights reserved. No part of this book may be reproduced or transmitted in any form or by any means, electronic or mechanical, including photocopying, recording, or by any information storage and retrieval system, without permission in writing from the copyright owner.

This is a work of fiction. Names, characters, places and incidents either are the product of the author's imagination or are used fictitiously, and any resemblance to any actual persons, living or dead, events, or locales is entirely coincidental.

Any people depicted in stock imagery provided by Getty Images are models, and such images are being used for illustrative purposes only.
Certain stock imagery © Getty Images.

Print information available on the last page.

Rev. date: 07/29/2020

To order additional copies of this book, contact:
Xlibris
1-888-795-4274
www.Xlibris.com
Orders@Xlibris.com
814815

Contents

Chapter 1	The Trial	1
Chapter 2	The Verdict	7
Chapter 3	Life Goes On	11
Chapter 4	Returning to School	15
Chapter 5	The Life of a Registered Nurse	19
Chapter 6	Changes and Choices	23
Chapter 7	The Meeting	27
Chapter 8	The Second Date	33
Chapter 9	Angelina Tells Her Story	39
Chapter 10	The First Goodbye	43
Chapter 11	Angelina Blooms	47
Chapter 12	Angelina's Happiness	51
Chapter 13	Police get involved	57
Chapter 14	Angelina Awakens	61
Chapter 15	A Night on the Town	65
Chapter 16	Awaiting Adam's Return	69
Chapter 17	Waiting to Hear	73
Chapter 18	Adam's Return	77
Chapter 19	Angelina's Desire	81
Chapter 20	Surrender	87
Chapter 21	Vandalism	91

Chapter 22	Getting Ready for the Trip	95
Chapter 23	The New York Trip Begins	99
Chapter 24	Thanksgiving Eve	103
Chapter 25	Thanksgiving	111
Chapter 26	The Shopping Trip	115
Chapter 27	Exploring New York City	119
Chapter 28	Back to Cape Girardeau	123
Chapter 29	Return to New York	127
Chapter 30	The Holidays with Adam	131
Chapter 31	Wedding Planning	135
Chapter 32	The King of Hearts Escapes	139
Chapter 33	Christmas and New Year's	145
Chapter 34	More Fun and Games	149
Chapter 35	Mr. and Mrs. Adam Harris	153
Chapter 36	The Endgame	157
Chapter 37	The Final Journey	163

About The Author 167

Dedicated to old friends and loved ones

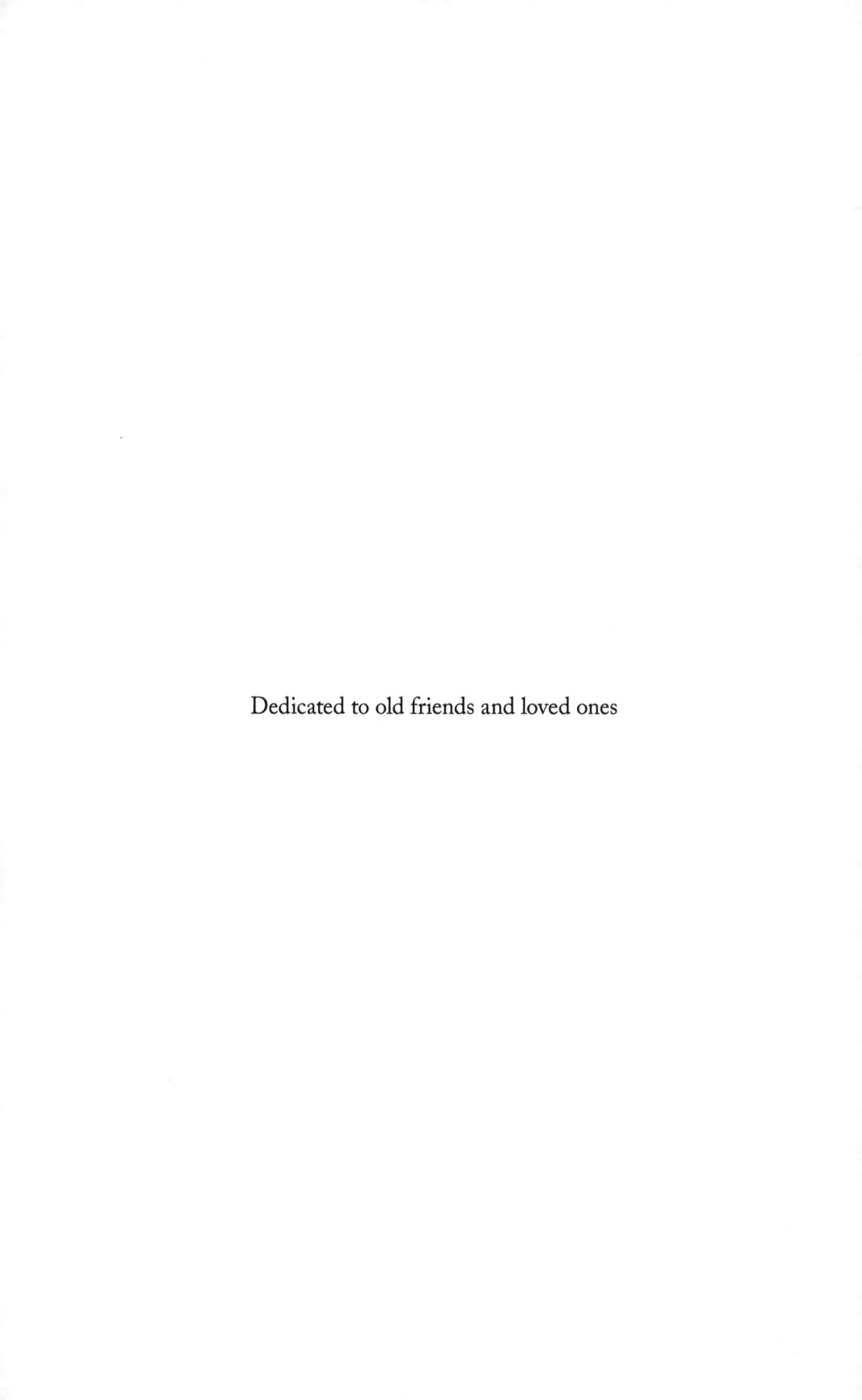

Chapter One

The Trial

Angelina Harper sat in the back of the Cape Girardeau County Courthouse courtroom. She arrived early so she could sit in the back row in the corner behind the defendant section. She wore a navy blue skirt, a white blouse, navy blue shoes, and a navy blue large-brimmed hat with a white bow. She also was wearing sunglasses. Angelina had put all of her long black hair up under her hat, hoping that no one would recognize her. She arrived early, hoping to avoid news reporters. She was anxious for the trial to start, but then again, she dreaded all the media attention. She just wanted her life to get back to normal if that was possible.

Angelina was beautiful at the age of twenty, even more beautiful than when she was in high school. The man on trial had stalked Angelina for four years and had murdered seven young men who were her boyfriends through high school. Her teenage years had been traumatic, to say the least, and Angelina had begun to realize that her life would never be the same or normal. It was an odd feeling knowing that events in one's life can have such a dramatic and profound impact. Angelina fought back tears as she waited for the trial to begin. She was dreading being called as the first witness at the trial. The prosecuting attorney had worked with her in preparation for her testimony, but Angelina was still emotional and afraid.

Angelina's parents had wanted to come with her to the trial to provide her with emotional support, but Angelina did not want them there. She felt this was something she had to do on her own. She did not want her parents to have to listen to all the gory details. Angelina felt if she could do this all on her own she would become stronger. At the age of twenty, Angelina was almost an adult and wanted to take care of herself.

As people began to file into the courtroom, Angelina felt some relief that no one seemed to recognize her. The prosecuting attorney recognized her as he entered the courtroom. He smiled and nodded in her direction as he went to the front of the room. Angelina recognized some of the parents of the boys that had been killed. They did not appear to recognize her though. A few news reporters came in also. No cameras were allowed.

Right before the judge appeared, a man in a dark suit was brought in by the county sheriff. Angelina's heart began to pound in her ears, and she immediately put her head down, hoping he would not recognize her. That was not the case. He stood at his attorney's table, staring at her with a big, awful smile on his face. Several people in the courtroom noticed and turned to see who he was smiling at. Angelina wanted to die, but she maintained her composure. She next heard a man with a loud voice say, "All rise." The judge entered the room just as she expected and had seen on television when she had watched *Perry Mason* shows. He was announced as the Honorable Judge Bartlet.

Angelina relaxed a little as the proceedings began with jury selection. That took the better part of the morning. Finally, seven men and five women were seated in the jury box. Angelina did not know any of them.

The judge asked the prosecuting attorney if he was ready to present his case. He answered that he was.

"Then call your first witness," said the judge.

"I call Angelina Harper," said the prosecuting attorney.

The audience started whispering and turned to look at her when she stood up. The judge used his gavel and said, "Quiet in the courtroom."

Angelina was sworn in and sat down in the witness chair. She then removed her sunglasses and looked at the prosecuting attorney as she waited for her first question. He asked her to state her name.

"My name is Angelina Harper," she said in a quivering voice.

Angelina was asked her age and where she lived. She was then asked a series of questions about when her stalking began and how she realized it was a stalker. She had to talk about each of the young men who had been killed and her relationship to them. She had to describe receiving the king of hearts playing cards, the sympathy cards sent to her by the stalker after each murder. She described how the playing cards appeared everywhere she seemed to go, including at her house, at school, and on her car. She described her fear and pain with each murder. She talked about the four years she had worked with the police trying to identify the killer and how her life had been an emotional roller coaster. The prosecuting attorney presented the large box of king of hearts playing cards, sympathy cards, and gifts she had received over the four years of her ordeal. Angelina cried when she saw them all and had to identify them. When she was presented with the tiny silver charm bracelet that had been stolen from her house, Angelina broke down. She was given a few minutes to compose herself and have a drink of water. She stated that it was a Christmas present from her first boyfriend.

Angelina's testimony went into the second day of the trial. The worst was when she had to answer the accusing questions of the defendant's attorney. She had been warned about this, and she waited before responding to each question to see if the prosecuting attorney would object. The prosecuting attorney exploded when the defense attorney implied that Angelina had led the stalker on. The debate between attorneys went on for several minutes, and Angelina was trembling with anger.

Finally, her cross-examination was over, and Angelina got up to leave the witness stand. As she passed between the prosecuting attorney and the defense attorney, she felt the murderer stand up, and he yelled at Angelina that she was his and he would always love her. The sheriff's deputy had to restrain John Noble, and the judge used his gavel, telling the man to sit down and that he would be physically restrained if he tried something like that again.

The trial continued for two weeks, and every day, Angelina had to be present. She hoped and prayed that she would not have to give more testimony. She listened to the testimony of Sergeant Jones, who had been the detective working with Angelina on this case for four years. She had to listen to how each of her seven boyfriends had been killed. During the testimony, Angelina wore her sunglasses. They were her only line of defense from all the people in the courtroom. From time to time, John Noble would turn in his seat to stare at Angelina. The sunglasses prevented him from seeing her eyes. The deputy always kept John Noble from looking at Angelina for very long. Each day when court was dismissed, the deputy had to restrain John Noble from getting to Angelina.

Finally, the trial was over. Little did Angelina know that that was just the beginning. The jury was given instructions for their deliberation, and they were dismissed to the jury room. The judge told them that their sequestration would continue until after they delivered a verdict. Sergeant Jones and another Cape Girardeau police officer escorted Angelina from the courtroom to her car to prevent reporters from mobbing her. That had been the routine every day after court was dismissed. Angelina was so grateful for their help. Every day John Noble would stand up and stare at Angelina as he was taken out of the courtroom. He always mumbled some words of love as he was escorted out. Angelina wanted to throw up.

Angelina went home and told her mom about the events of the day, just as she had done every day of the trial. Now the waiting for the verdict began.

Chapter Two

The Verdict

That night Angelina received a call about 6:00 p.m. from the court, stating a verdict had been reached by the jury. They instructed her to be back at the courthouse at 8:00 p.m. Angelina took a deep breath as she hung up the phone and told her parents. Because it was dark outside and because reporters would be waiting for her, Angelina's mom and dad insisted on accompanying her to the courthouse. That relieved some of Angelina's anxiety.

Angelina sat in the back of the courtroom as usual. She had her hat and sunglasses on. John Noble was escorted into the courtroom in shackles. He, of course, looked at Angelina and smiled. Next the attorneys and the judge came in. The jury was escorted into the jury box. Judge Bartlet called for order in the courtroom. He asked the jury if they had reached a verdict. An older gray-headed lady stood up and said, "We have, Your Honor." She handed the bailiff a piece of folded paper, which was taken to the judge. Angelina started to tremble. The judge read what was on the paper, then asked for John Noble to stand and face the jury. His attorney stood with him. The little old lady read the verdict.

"We the jury find the defendant, John Noble, guilty of murder in the first degree for the seven murders he was accused of."

The judge ask each juror to state their verdict separately.

A roar came up from the courtroom and reporters sped out of the courtroom to report on the verdict. John Noble turned to Angelina and said this didn't change anything and that he was still in love with her and would never let her go. The judge used his gavel and said "Quiet in the courtroom." The judge said that court would resume again in the morning for the formal sentencing at 9:00 a.m. He used his gavel again and said, "Court dismissed."

The bailiff said "All rise" as the judge left the courtroom. For Angelina, the trial was still not over. She knew she had to be present tomorrow for the sentencing discussion. She had been told that she and all the victim's families would be allowed to speak to the murderer and the court about their feelings regarding their sentencing wishes for John Noble. That would be another exhausting day for Angelina.

There was a mob of reporters outside the courthouse that swarmed Angelina and her parents. Thankfully there were police officers who maintained control of the crowd and protected Angelina and her parents as they got into their car to drive away. Angelina did not want to talk to any of them.

Angelina told her mom and dad, "I don't think this will ever be over for me." She started to sob.

Angelina was so tired that she went straight to bed and went immediately to sleep. It was a restless sleep and was disturbed by dreams of John Noble chasing her.

The next morning, Angelina dressed in what she had planned to wear to court that day. She wanted to wear the same outfit she wore the first day of the trial: the navy blue skirt, white blouse, navy shoes, the navy blue large-brimmed hat with the white bow, and sunglasses. She arrived early and sat in the same spot she had sat in every day. She kept her head down just she always had.

When court finally convened, each family member of the seven young men who had been killed spoke about the anguish they had experienced when their son was killed and the anger they felt when the murderer was not known. Angelina cried through all these speeches and heard each family member say they didn't want John Noble to ever see the light of day. Some said they wanted him to be put to death in the electric chair. Angelina was a nervous wreck when it was her time to speak. She felt everyone's eyes follow her to the front of the courtroom. With a trembling voice, she began to speak.

"Your honor, I have lived with the horror that John Noble caused for the last five years. I have lived in fear and don't believe I will ever be the same carefree girl I once was. I had looked forward to my teenage years, dating, going to football games and dances. Each of the young boys I dated were wonderful young men, and I am sorry that they died because of John Noble's deranged obsession with me. I didn't realize I was being stalked at first and every boy I talked with was in danger. I know in my heart that if these boys had lived, I might have someday married one of them. I remember each of them fondly. Now I don't know that I will ever be strong enough again to date or marry. I don't believe I will ever be free of John Noble, so I can only wish that he be locked away in some hole somewhere and that I never see him or hear his name again. He has taken away my youth and my possibilities."

Angelina turned and was walking back to her seat when John Noble stood up and said, "Angelina, you don't mean what you say. I love you, and you will never be free of me. This will never be over."

The judge again had to call for order in the court. He asked for John Noble to stand for his sentencing. The judge said, "It is the decision of this court that you be sentenced to seven life sentences for the murders you have committed. They will be served consecutively, and there will be no possibility of parole. Mr. Noble do you have anything to say?"

John Noble smiled and shook his head no and gave out a menacing loud laugh. He turned to Angelina and said, "Angelina, you will never be rid of me."

With that, John Noble was led out of the courtroom and out of Angelina's sight. A cold shiver went down her spine. Will she ever be able to forget? Would she ever truly be free of John Noble? She believed at that point that she would never be free again, would never look forward to love and marriage as she had anticipated with excitement when she was a teenager, would never be safe and happy again. How would she ever be able to cope with life? A lonely feeling spread across her that accentuated the loneliness she was just beginning to experience

Chapter Three

Life Goes On

For the next few weeks, Angelina was extremely quiet and kept to herself. The phone at home seemed to be ringing constantly. On the other line were news reporters wanting to talk with her. There continued to be articles in the *Southeast Missourian* newspaper every day about the trial, the verdict, and John Noble. She just wished this all would stop. Angelina did not go out in public. She did take long drives in the country just to find some relaxation and peace. She was thinking about what she was going to do with the rest of her life.

On one of these drives she stopped at a small-town grocery store. There was an old man sitting outside. He watched as she approached. When she stepped up onto the porch to go inside for a soda, the old man said, "It's good to see you, Angelina. I am Henry Miesner, an old friend of your grandfather. I haven't seen you since you were a young girl. I know you have been through a lot, but you are always welcome here."

At that moment Angelina realized she was in Farrar, Missouri, where her grandparents had lived and raised their twelve children, one of whom was Angelina's mother. It seemed that Angelina, without realizing it, had returned to her roots. Everything came into focus now, and Angelina felt peace that she had not experienced since she was a child visiting her grandparents on their farm on weekends.

Angelina sat down beside the old man and began to ask questions about her grandparents' farm and the town.

"The old farm house and barn are still standing. As you can see, the general store is still here where you came every Saturday to buy your bag of candy. The church and school are still at the top of the hill. Other than that, this old town hasn't changed much. We still only have about two hundred residents. Did you come here to visit your grandma and grandpa's graves? You know your Uncle Martin is buried there too. He was only twelve years old when he died from a ruptured appendix. They didn't have surgery available back then that would have saved his life."

"I think I am going to visit their graves since I am here."

After a little more conversation, Angelina told Mr. Miesner goodbye and that it was nice seeing him again.

"Come back again. You can usually find me sitting on this porch, just passing the time away."

Angelina drank the rest of her soda and waved goodbye to the old man as she drove up the hill to the cemetery. There she found her grandma and grandpa's graves. She stood there for quite a while just thinking of her carefree days as a child visiting them on the farm. She next set about finding her uncle Martin's grave. While standing at his grave, she surveyed the other gravestones close by and saw the grave of Sara Turner, who had been murdered in Farrar in 1953. That murder case had put Farrar, Missouri, on the map. Oddly enough, Angelina felt a closeness to Sara Turner. She had also been through an awful lot at such a young age.

As Angelina left the cemetery and was driving away, Angelina said to herself that she would return to this place of peace often to visit the old man and the cemetery. She would bring flowers the next time. Angelina waved to the old man on the porch of Eggers General store as she drove by and looked toward her grandparents' farmhouse as she drove out of Farrar. There was a smile on Angelina's face as she drove home. She continued to think about her future. She knew she needed to make a decision about what she was going to do with her life and get on with it, but for now, she just needed to be free and get some badly needed rest.

When Angelina got home, she told her mom where she had been and how enjoyable it was to be in Farrar. "I intend to go back and visit Mr. Miesner. He made me feel at home, and I was at peace there for those few hours."

"That is great, darling. It can be your special hideaway."

"While on the drive home, I began to think about what I needed to do with my life. I thought about maybe just getting a job to occupy my time," Angelina said.

"Oh no, Angelina. You need to follow your dream and go back to school to become a nurse. You are young and need to be around people your own age. There is always time to work later, and you need to work in a career that you can love."

"Well, I just wanted you to know I am thinking about my future. I will make a decision soon."

That night Angelina could not sleep. She thought about the last four years, the trial, and John Noble. She prayed that God would give her strength to carry on with her life and for him to help her make a decision about her future.

The days turned into weeks, and Angelina finally decided to go back to school for her nursing degree. She knew that would occupy her time, and she might enjoy meeting new people. She told her mom and dad, and that seemed to please them. She went up to Southeast Missouri State College and visited with the nursing department chair. She was immediately accepted back into the program. She would be starting back to school in August of 1967.

The rest of the summer, Angelina was free to get ready for school. There was shopping to do for some new clothes. Angelina felt some loneliness, but that was welcomed. She read some books that helped her pass the time. It was odd, but Angelina was content to be alone. It seemed like all of her high school friends had gone in different directions. Some were at different colleges, some were working, and some were already married. Angelina vowed that she would just have to make some new girlfriends once school started. She would be with other nursing students, and that promised to be an adventure. Strangely enough, Angelina no longer thought as much about boys. It was as though the curse of John Noble still haunted her. Deep in her heart, she knew it always would.

The highlight of Angelina's summer was when Elvis Presley returned home from the service and his comeback show was on television. Angelina loved Elvis's music, and he was so very handsome. She went the next day to the Town Plaza shopping center and bought some of his records.

Chapter Four

Returning to School

Angelina returned to college in the fall of 1967. She was to reenter the nursing program at Southeast Missouri State College. It was her sincere desire to pick up with her life where she had left off in 1966. She was accepted back into the freshman nursing class and was looking forward to meeting new people and being busy. She had realized over the last couple of weeks that she could not continue to live every day without purpose. All that did was to give Angelina too much time to think about John Noble and how he had stolen her youth. This made her avoid the public, and she was living without purpose.

School was starting in just a couple of weeks, and Angelina was already busy enrolling in her classes, getting her books, and putting together her wardrobe needs for school. She did make one last trip to Farrar, Missouri, to place flowers on her grandparent's graves and on the grave of Sara Turner, for whom she felt a kindred spirit. She also wanted to visit one last time with Henry Miesner. He had been so kind and understanding and made her feel at peace with herself after the trial. As she drove by Egger's General store, Mr. Miesner was not sitting on the porch as he usually did. She stopped and went inside the store to inquire about him and found that he had recently passed away. Angelina suddenly felt a sadness rush over her. He was such a nice man.

Angelina continued her drive up the hill to the Salem Church Cemetery. She laid white roses on her grandparents' graves, saving four roses for Mr. Miesner. She laid six yellow roses on Sara Turner's grave and proceeded to find Mr. Miesner's grave and laid the remaining white roses on his still-fresh grave. She stood at his grave a few minutes to say a prayer. Before she left his grave site, she said, "Thank you, Mr. Miesner, for being my friend and listening to me when I needed someone to talk to. I will miss our long talks on the store porch and will never forget you."

Angelina drove home, thinking about the world she lived in and all the death that seemed to occur every day. The Vietnam War was raging and was taking young men's lives every day. Some of them she had gone to high school with. The number of American soldiers killed each day was announced on the nightly news. It was depressing. There were war protesters everywhere. There were sit-ins and sing-ins, and many young men were burning their draft cards. It was all so depressing. There was too much death in this world. Angelina wanted peace and to save lives and not take lives. Becoming a nurse would help Angelina meet that goal.

School was starting in a week. Angelina seemed to have more purpose now. However, Angelina received a letter in the mail before school started. When she opened it, she found it was from John Noble. Would he ever leave her alone? It was a rambling love letter. She took it to her mother, who immediately called Sergeant Jones at the police department. He told her he would call the prison in Jefferson City to talk with the warden to see if they could stop John Noble from harassing Angelina and keep him from mailing her more letters. He instructed Angelina's mother to write on any future letters that might slip through "Return to Sender" and throw them in the mailbox. Fear immediately returned to Angelina, and that night, sleep evaded her. "What next?" questioned Angelina.

The news media continued to pursue Angelina, wanting an interview. She kept avoiding them. She told them she wanted to be left alone, but they never seemed to take no for an answer. They were like vultures. Once she was in school, she knew she could avoid the press and concentrate on her studies. Anyway, that was her hope.

School started the middle of August. Angelina walked to school as she did in 1966, but she took a different route to the college. She did not want to walk by John Noble's old house or walk by the tennis courts where he once hung king of hearts playing cards on the fencing. It was like she was turning over a new leaf. The nursing department classes were held in the basement of Academic Hall. There was an office area, two classrooms, and a clinical lab where the students would practice nursing skills before going into the hospital. Her first semester, she had a nursing class called Professional Development. It met for one hour each week. All the freshman nursing students met together in that class. There were sixty-five freshman nursing students in the class. Every week, the class size seemed to get smaller. Angelina had heard that the nursing program was tough and had many dropouts, but Angelina was determined she would not be a dropout. Angelina spent many hours studying either at home or in the library between classes.

Angelina made many friends in the nursing program. They did not know about her high school saga, and she never brought it up. She just wanted to be herself. There were no male nursing students, and Angelina didn't have many men in her other classes. No guys showed much interest in Angelina. That was probably because Angelina lived off campus and was not a flirt or party animal. The nursing students also stood out on campus. It was the age of the miniskirt, but the nursing students had to wear dresses that came below the knee. They just looked like student nuns. Who wanted to be seen with them?

One summer, Angelina had microbiology class with a cute guy who was friendly and outgoing. He flirted with her some, and she did the same, but he was in a fraternity and lived on campus. Angelina simply wasn't ready for any kind of a relationship. She wasn't certain she would ever be ready to go down that road again. When the summer was over, she never had another class with him. Her fellow nursing-student friends set Angelina up a couple of times with guys, but she just wasn't interested. Was she afraid? Had she lost the enthusiasm she once had for boys? Angelina just felt dead inside. Maybe once she was out of nursing school and more time had passed, the enthusiasm would return. Only time would tell. For now Angelina was content with her world the way it was.

Angelina continued to receive cards and letters from John Noble. She continue to send them back unopened. The news media finally slowed down on their constant pursuit to interview her. They only appeared on the anniversary of the murder victims' deaths. Angelina's friends gradually learned about Angelina's high school experiences and understood why she was the way she was. They accepted her the way she was, and they always included her when they went out. For that, Angelina was grateful.

Angelina graduated from nursing school in August of 1969 with an associate of arts degree in nursing. That entitled her to set for her license as a registered professional nurse. The only thing that scared her was that she had to travel to Jefferson City to take the exams. That was where John Noble was imprisoned. She didn't like the idea of being that close to him. Somehow she would have to endure and keep her mind on the exams.

Chapter Five

The Life of a Registered Nurse

Angelina Harper passed her state board exams with flying colors. Of the original sixty-five nursing students she started school with, only eleven graduated. That was a feat of its own. She looked at her new name tag as she got dressed for work her first day for work. It looked strange to see 'Angelina Harper, RN.' She wore her uniform and name tag with pride as she walked into the hospital that morning, carrying her nursing cap that she would put on once she reached the orientation classroom. Her first day on the job would be spent in orientation—as if eight hours of orientation would be enough time to learn all she needed to know about the hospital. The rest of the week would be spent in observation on her assigned nursing unit.

Angelina was scheduled to staff the evening shift from 3:00 p.m. to 11:00 p.m. Even though she wasn't looking forward to having to walk to her car at night, she thought she would enjoy having daylight hours free. She would be able to sleep in, go shopping, and sunbathe if she wanted. She learned her job quickly. She had to because she was the only RN on the floor on the evening shift. Thank God for experienced nursing assistants who kept her informed about what the needs of the patients were. When it was time for supper, she would tell them where in the hospital she was going for supper so they could call her if needed. That was how it worked in those days.

If the evening shift was like most, she would take report on the patients at the beginning of the shift. If she got to work early, she would get a head start by pouring her medications ahead of time. That was a chore because the cabinet at the nurse's station housed big bottles of medications organized in alphabetical order. The only problem was they were according to generic names instead of trade names. She had to know both. One day her head nurse asked her why she came in so early. When Angelina explained, the head nurse said she wished she wouldn't arrive early. Angelina snapped back, "You should be happy that I'm here."

After she received a report from the day nurse on all the patients, the two of them would count the narcotics in the locked drawer. Hopefully, it came out right. If anything was missing, it was a major deal until the missing drug was found. Usually, the day nurse merely forgot to sign out the drug when she got in the drawer to get something out for pain for a patient. That often was not easy to find on a floor of thirty-five patients though. If the mistake was not easily found, the pharmacist had to be called, and a report had to be filled out. Regardless, the day nurse could not go home until the error was rectified.

Angelina loved patient care. Every patient was different, and on a medical floor like hers, a nurse's assessment skills were vitally important. Angelina became very good at assessing what was going on with her patients. If her assessment was wrong, a patient could be quickly in trouble. The physicians respected Angelina, and they trusted her judgment, knowing she would call them if something was going wrong with their patients.

All of the physicians and staff knew Angelina's story and knew she kept pretty well to herself and was all about her nursing responsibilities when she was at work. She was not flirtatious as she worked with doctors and other males at the hospital. Everyone seemed to know why she was the way she was. When new male employees came to work at the hospital, they often wondered why Angelina was so aloof. They would attempt to flirt with her until finally someone would inform them that Angelina had a story that made her the way she was. They would then quickly loose interest. Even though Angelina was beautiful, by the time that Angelina was in her twenties, most young men had lost interest.

After two years of working on the medical floor, the director of Nursing at the hospital approached Angelina about working in Intensive Care. Angelina was hesitant, saying "Everyone is dying back there." The director pressured Angelina until she finally agreed to give it a try but said, "Now if I don't like it, you have to let me come back to my spot on this floor." Once Angelina was oriented to ICU, she loved it, and she stayed. Because Angelina was so good at patient assessment, she was able to keep patients from getting into trouble, and she saved many patient lives. She loved the excitement of working there because she never knew what would happen next and she was learning so much. The doctors took the time to teach the nurses in Intensive Care when they were there.

Nurses in the ICU had to respond to code blues or cardiac arrests as they occurred in the hospital. It was a great feeling whenever a patient was brought back to life from the edge of death. Angelina actually looked forward to going to work in the ICU every day. The reputation of the nurses working in ICU was that they were the best of the best.

In 1975, Angelina's father died suddenly of a heart attack. One day he was planting tomato plants in his garden in the backyard and the next day he died in the very intensive care unit that Angelina worked in. Luckily Angelina was off work that day and was not there when he came in and coded. Her father was only fifty-eight years old. It was a crushing loss for Angelina and her mother. Angelina was still living at home. She had thought a lot about getting her own apartment, but now she knew she needed to continue living at home for her mother's sake. Angelina was not looking forward to living alone since John Harper was sending her letters and seemed to know her every move. He still was a threatening figure that seemed to be in her life forever. Fear was always with Angelina, and she could never get over the feeling of being watched and followed. How could that be? Regardless, the King of Hearts seemed to know what was going on in Angelina's life.

In 1978, Angelina's mother died of a broken heart. Her mother and father had been so close that her mom could not face life without him. She stopped eating after Angelina's dad died. She started drinking beer and became reclusive in the house. Angelina would come home from work and find all the house curtains shut and find the food she had fixed for her mom not eaten. When Angelina would ask her mom why she was not getting over her depression and was drinking so much, she would say, "I just want to be down there with your dad," meaning she wanted to be at the cemetery with her dad. Now Angelina was alone, and she had to make some decisions. None of the choices were appealing, especially since the King of Hearts knew she was now alone. He had sent her a sympathy card when each of her parents died

Chapter Six

Changes and Choices

After Angelina's parents were both gone, Angelina had to make some decisions about her life going forward. She was an only child, so she inherited everything. Should she continue to live in the family home alone or sell the property and move into an apartment? Keeping the home meant a lot of upkeep and responsibility. She was working full-time and did have time to mow the yard and see after the problems that a house brought with it. Angelina decided to sell the home and the majority of its contents. Finding an apartment where she would feel safe and secure was a major concern. Fear seemed to take over her life again, but she began the hunt for an apartment where she could take refuge. After a few weeks, Angelina found a spacious two-bedroom apartment in a good part of town. The locks on the door were dead-bolt type, and the door was heavy. The windows had strong security locks, and she was on the second floor.

The family home sold without too much difficulty except she had to finance the sale and accept monthly payments from the buyer for the next twenty years. The United States was in a period of extreme inflation, and interest rates were at 18 per cent. To say the least, no one could afford that kind of interest. Angelina carried the loan for 15 percent interest, which was better than the banks could offer. The added monthly income was going to help pay for Angelina's apartment.

Angelina thought she might rid her life of the King of Hearts by moving to an apartment. Maybe he would not know where she moved and would stop sending her letters and would stop knowing her every move. It was all wishful thinking. At least Angelina was working the day shift now and did not get off work any later than eleven thirty at night. The only problem was that the King of Hearts had managed to follow her into her work. The hospital had what was called interdepartmental mail, and she would occasionally receive a piece of mail in one of these yellow mailers with her name on it. It was always a king of hearts playing card. So her stalker was either working at the hospital, or he had figured out how to inject a mailer into the floor-to-floor system. Maybe it was just a prankster at the hospital who knew Angelina's story. Regardless, Angelina did not find it amusing.

Angelina went to her director of Nursing, hoping they could trace the mailers coming to the ICU and catch the person, but the attempts proved fruitless. Many times Angelina would find a king of hearts playing card on the windshield of her car or taped to her apartment door. She would tear them off and throw them on the ground. She would speed into her apartment and lock her doors. She hated John Noble and his ghostly stalker. Angelina finally purchased some Mace to carry with her for self-protection. She thought about purchasing a gun but knew that it was illegal to carry it into the hospital. She often kept her curtains closed if she was home alone during the day, and then she realized that she was becoming reclusive like her mom had been. Angelina knew then that her mom had merely been afraid of living alone. Angelina did not want to live like her mom and be afraid of living alone. She decided to take self-protection lessons. She enjoyed those classes. She met new people who didn't know her story, and she had a feeling of belonging since the classes were mostly women. They were mostly single women who also feared living alone. Angelina would often go out with these women after class, and she really enjoyed their company. Eventually Angelina told them her story about John Noble since they all opened up and shared their lives with her. Some of the women were divorced and were afraid of their ex-husbands. Angelina learned that they were all in this together.

Over a short period, Angelina earned her black belt in karate. She continued to train because she didn't want to lose her skills or her new friends. Angelina was even more beautiful. She had an even more beautiful figure as a result of her training. She also began to laugh and smile more. Everyone at work noticed the change in Angelina. Angelina's confidence in herself soared. Angelina even began to go out at night with friends without fear. Occasionally, someone from town or high school would recognize Angelina and say, "Aren't you Angelina Harper?" Her friends would gather around Angelina just as Angelina did when one of them were approached by a stranger.

Eventually everyone at work learned that Angelina had a black belt in karate. Maybe it was her imagination, but she seemed to have more respect. They all new that Angelina could take care of herself and she was strong. It didn't seem to affect the King of Hearts though. The cards and letters kept coming. John Noble mentioned in one of his letters that he knew she had a black belt, and he informed her that it wouldn't do her any good if he ever got out. That sent a shiver down Angelina's spine. Little did Angelina know that this was just the beginning of her journey.

Chapter Seven

The Meeting

It was Friday, November 10, 1979. Angelina was working in the intensive care unit, and it was not particularly busy that day. Dr. Alan Spindler had come into the unit to see one of his patients. He was accompanied by another man whom Angelina did not know. She went about her work with her patients since Dr. Spindler's patient was being cared for by another nurse in the unit. As Angelina walked by the nurses' station she spoke to Dr. Spindler.

"Alan, who is that stunningly beautiful woman?" the stranger asked.

"You must mean Angelina Harper."

"Yes. I want you to introduce me to her. What do you know about her? Is she married?"

"She's not married, but she has a story," Alan said.

"Well, what's the story?"

"It's too long to tell now. I think I should let her tell you. Ms. Harper, may I speak to you a moment?

"Yes, Dr. Spindler?"

"I want to introduce you to a friend of mine. Angelina Harper, this is

Adam Harris. Adam, this is Angelina Harper, the nurse manager of this ICU," said Dr. Spindler.

"It's nice to meet you, Dr. Harris."

"Ms. Harper, Adam is not a physician. He is a corporate attorney from New York City. He handles my medical group's affairs."

"I see. I thought maybe you were a new physician that I had not yet met," Angelina replied.

"Ms. Harper, I have a favor to ask. My wife and I are hosting a dinner party for Adam tonight since he is in town, and I would like to invite you to act as Adam's date so he is not the odd man out. Otherwise all our wives will ignore us and monopolize all of Adam's time."

"I can speak for myself, Alan. Would you let me take you to this evening dinner, Angelina? I promise to take care of you."

Angelina smiled and said yes before she realized what she was doing. What made her say yes after so many young men had asked her out and she always turned them down? Was this because Adam Harris was tall, dark, and handsome? Was it because Angelina was mesmerized by his dark-brown eyes or his deep, mellow voice? Maybe it was because Angelina was lonely and she trusted Alan Spindler. He had a good reputation in the hospital and had always been kind to Angelina. Maybe it was because Adam Harris promised to take care of her, and she suddenly felt safe. Regardless, Adam Harris looked handsome in a suit, and she said yes without thinking twice.

"Excellent. I will pick you up at 6:30 p.m. All I need is your address."

Angelina scribbled her address on a piece of paper, and they parted, leaving Angelina a little weak in the knees. She gathered herself and began to think about her patient's need again.

The rest of the day went rather quickly. Angelina overheard a couple of the other staff whispering that Angelina had a date. She was sure it would be all over the hospital and hoped no one would ask her about it. The facade that Angelina had constructed for herself over the years was crumbling a little.

When Angelina got off work, she went home and started getting ready for this date. Her hands seemed to be trembling. She had to figure out what she might wear. A dinner party was formal, and she had only one black cocktail dress. When she put it on, she looked in the mirror and thought it fit her perfectly. She had worn it earlier in the year to a hospital event. It still looked good. Angelina let her hair down and dried it. It fell around her shoulders. She always wore her hair up when at work. That didn't hide all of her beauty, but she looked more aloof when it was up. She wondered if Adam Harris would notice that her hair was down. She applied her makeup and stood in front of the mirror, looking at herself. She felt good about the way she looked. Angelina applied a light-red lipstick. She thought to herself she was still beautiful. Just then the doorbell rang.

She went to the door and looked through the peephole. It was Adam Harris, and he was right on time. She took a deep breath and opened the door.

"Hello, Adam."

"Good evening, Angelina. You look beautiful. I didn't realize your hair was so long. It must have been all piled up under your nursing cap."

"Does it look OK?" asked Angelina. "I can put it up if you like it better that way."

"Absolutely not. It is lovely," said Adam. "Are you ready to go? Let me help you with your coat."

As they exited the apartment, Adam noticed a fifty-dollar bill lying on the end table by the door. He thought that was odd. Angelina locked her door carefully. The door had two dead-bolt locks.

Adam Harris looked so handsome in his dark suit. His cologne as not strong but smelled good. Angelina spoke first and asked him to tell her about himself.

"Well, as you know, I am from New York City."

"What brings you to Cape Girardeau?" Angelina asked.

"My mother was born and raised in Cape Girardeau. She met my dad when she was away at college. He was an attorney also and, in fact, started the business. I would come home with my mom to Cape Girardeau in the summer to see my grandparents. I always loved his town. That is how I met a lot of prominent doctors, lawyers, and business men here. Once I graduated from law school, they hired me and my dad's law firm to handle their affairs."

"Where did you go to law school?"

"Harvard," Adam replied. "Well, it looks like we are here. You'll have to tell me your story on the way home."

Angelina said, "I'm afraid we won't have enough time." Angelina looked at Dr. Spindler's house and said, "How beautiful. It is enormous."

Adam help Angelina from the car, took her arm, and guided her to the front door. They were met by Mrs. Spindler as the butler took her coat. "Good evening, Adam. This must be Angelina Harper?"

"Yes, ma'am."

"Angelina, call me Sarah. Let's join the others."

Angelina recognized the others in Alan Spindler's group. She did not know their wives. They looked at her strangely. Angelina hoped it was because she was with Adam and not because they knew her past story. Either way, she was certain that Adam noticed. Even so, Angelina was cordial as she was introduced to the group. Adam got Angelina a glass of wine, and they all sat in the living room, awaiting supper. One of the wives sitting next to Angelina said, "Angelina, I haven't heard anything about you for several years since the trial. I didn't know you were a nurse."

"Yes, I got my nursing license and began working at the hospital in 1969."

Adam knew that this made Angelina uncomfortable, and he put his arm around her in a protective gesture and felt Angelina trembling. Just then the butler announced that dinner was served. Adam kept his arm around her as he led her into the dining room. Thank goodness Dr. Spindler was sitting beside her and Adam. She wouldn't have to endure any more questions from that woman.

The food was delicious, and Angelina enjoyed the conversation with Adam and Dr. Spindler. The event was over almost as fast as it started. Someone said, after going back to the living room, it had begun to snow outside. Adam got up to look outside with the rest of the men. Angelina excused herself to go to the ladies' room. When she returned, she heard two women talking about her. She didn't think Adam had heard them though. Angelina wanted to cry.

Adam came up to her with a smile and said it was snowing quite heavily, and he thought they should go. Angelina agreed. Angelina went to Mrs. Spindler and thanked her for a lovely evening. Angelina and Adam went out into the night. The snow was whipping round. Angelina almost fell but Adam caught her

"I told you I wouldn't let anything happen to you, Angelina."

Angelina laughed and said, "I now have proof of that promise."

"You know, Angelina, Alan told me you had a story. You are going to have to tell me. I am a good listener. Obviously, some of the wives were prying into you story and that made you uncomfortable. I felt you trembling when I put my arm around you."

"My story is a long one, and I don't want to talk about it tonight. I don't want to ruin a perfectly lovely date."

Adam took her hand and said he understood.

Adam walked Angelina to her door, and she unlocked the door. She turned to Adam and said, "I have a favor to ask. Would you go into my apartment and turn on the lights in all the rooms?"

"Will do."

When Adam returned, he said, "All's well." He stood in front of Angelina and looked into her eyes. "I want to see you tomorrow. I will call you in the morning, and maybe we can go to lunch. First, I want to kiss you good night."

Before she knew it, Adam kissed her. She went weak in her knees. It had been a very long time since Angelina had been kissed. It was a good thing that Adam was holding her by her shoulders or she would have fallen. He smiled as if he knew. Angelina wrote her telephone number on his hand, and as he left her doorway, Angelina noticed a king of hearts playing card taped to her door. She tore it off and threw it on the ground and said, "Good night, Adam."

Adam heard her lock her door and bent down to pick up the card as he walked off. He was intrigued with Angelina and was anxious to see her again.

Chapter Eight

The Second Date

Angelina's mind was racing as she got ready for bed. She had had a wonderful evening with Adam Harris. She surprised herself by being relaxed with him. As she crawled into bed, she wondered if he would really call her in the morning. He did say he wanted to see her again, and he gave her that good-night kiss. Angelina thought about that kiss. It had been at least ten years since her last kiss. She could hardly remember it. She didn't think she had ever felt like this about any kiss before.

Why had she avoided dating anyone all these years since John Noble had been sent to prison? He had succeeded in ruining her life, but she had allowed that to happen because of her fears and insecurities. This new stalker was just reporting her activities to John Noble so that he could continue to harass her from behind bars. Adam Harris was the kind of man she could feel safe with. As Angelina drifted off to sleep, she decided to see where the dating of Adam Harris might take her. Either way, she knew she was not going to turn down dates anymore. She had wasted too many years fearing the King of Hearts. She was tired of being lonely.

Angelina slept well and awoke with a smile on her face. Her first thoughts were about Adam Harris and their date last night. She felt giddy like a schoolgirl. *He is so handsome*, she thought. What did he ever see in her? About that time, her phone rang. She was still in bed, and it was nine o'clock. Angelina had never slept that late before.

"Hello," said Angelina.

"Good morning, beautiful," said Adam. "What are you doing?"

"Well, to tell you the truth, I woke up about thirty minutes ago and was just lounging around thinking. I can't believe I slept this late."

"I hope you were thinking about me," Adam said with a laugh.

"I was thinking about the good time I had last night."

"Are you ready to spend the day with me today?"

"Yes. What do you have in mind?"

"I'm going to keep that a surprise. Can I pick you up about eleven thirty?"

"OK."

"Dress casual but warm. There is still some snow on the ground, and it is cold," Adam said.

After she hung up the phone, Angelina jumped out of bed. She had only two hours to get ready. As she was scurrying around, the phone rang again. Did Adam forget to tell her something?

"Hello," said Angelina.

"Angelina, you are up to no good," said the male voice on the other end. "You are cheating on me, and it had better stop."

Angelina slammed the receiver down on the phone. Her hands were trembling. She had never received a call from the King of Hearts since he was in prison. He knew of her date last night. His spy must have told him.

Angelina looked at the phone and yelled, "Screw you!" She then started to get ready for her date with Adam. That call was not going to ruin her day.

Angelina looked at herself in the mirror. She decided to wear a pair of black slacks, a red sweater, and a pair of black boots. Maybe today she wouldn't fall and make a fool of herself like she did last night, trying to walk in the snow in heels. Holding onto Adam helped her maintain her balance. She wasn't afraid when he caught her in his arms. Just then the doorbell rang.

Excitedly Angelina opened the door. There stood Adam with a red rose in his hand. Angelina smiled as she took it from Adam's hand to take a smell. "Thank you, Adam," she said. "It will just take a minute to put it in water."

As they were about to leave the apartment, Adam asked "Why do you have a fifty-dollar bill lying on the end table by your door?"

"My karate teacher told the class that it is a way to know if someone has been in your home while you are gone. No one can leave money when they see it."

"I see. I didn't know you were learning karate. Have you earned a belt yet?"

Angelina laughed and said she had a black belt.

Adam said, "Oh my! I had better watch my p's and q's. I am impressed."

"I'm sure you can take care of yourself just fine."

Angelina slid into the car as Adam opened her car door. It was then that Angelina realized that Adam's black car was a Mercedes. "This is a beautiful car. Is it yours, or is it a rental?"

"Thank you. It is mine. I only get to drive it when I am in Cape. It stays in the garage at my condo when I am in New York."

"Where are we going, Adam?"

"I thought I would take you to lunch at the Anvil in St. Genevieve. How does that sound?"

"That sounds wonderful. I have heard a lot about it, but I have never eaten there."

"I hope you like it. They are famous for their onion rings, among other things," said Adam.

"I don't think I need any of those. They will make my breath stink."

Adam laughed and said, "You don't want your breath to stink when I kiss you?"

Angelina blushed like a teenager.

Adam chuckled when he saw Angelina blush. "I haven't seen a woman blush in a very long time."

When they arrived at the Anvil, Adam took Angelina's hand to help her out of the car and kept holding it as they walked into the restaurant and were seated. Adam ordered the onion rings and smiled at Angelina. "I have gum in the car, and I will share it." Angelina blushed again. Since Angelina had never eaten there before, she ordered a salad.

Adam asked Angelina about her family. She told him her father was a laborer at the Florsheim Shoe Company in Cape. He was born and raised in Cape. Her mother was a stay-at-home mom. Angelina explained that she was an only child, so she was quite shy growing up. Angelina stated that her father died suddenly of a heart attack at the age of fifty-eight. Her mother died of a broken heart at the age of fifty-five. Angelina had a few aunts and uncles still living, but most of her cousins no longer lived nearby.

When the onion rings came to the table, Angelina was forced to try them. "Oh, they are delicious!"

"I knew you would like them," Adam said smiling at her.

After lunch they walked around the town square before heading back to Cape Girardeau. It seemed that they had a lot to talk about, and Angelina easily talked with Adam. When they arrived back in Cape, Adam asked if Angelina would like to see his apartment.

"I would love to see it."

When Adam opened the door to his apartment, Angelina was amazed at how huge it was. "Did you decorate this yourself? It is beautiful," Angelina said.

"No. I'm afraid I have no taste. Alan's wife did it for me. I have someone come in and clean it up after I leave town. Now Angelina, it is quiet here, and the view of the city is nice. I want you to sit down here and tell me your story. Alan told me you had one, but he would not tell me. He said that it was your story to tell. Does it have anything to do with this?" Adam took the king of hearts playing card from his pocket and placed it on the coffee table.

Chapter Nine

Angelina Tells Her Story

Angelina trembled a little and with a quivering voice said, "I don't know if I can. I haven't talked about this for a long time."

"Maybe it is time to talk more openly about it."

With a deep breath, Angelina began. "It started when I was about to enter my sophomore year of high school. I was looking forward to driving and going on dates like most sixteen-year-olds. I was sitting on my front porch at home one evening after supper as I did most evenings. I was thinking about going back to school when I noticed a king of hearts playing card hanging on the railing of my porch. I wondered who put it there and why. My mother thought it was a prank or a secret admirer. The next day, I went to my driver's education class at the high school. It was a summer school class that would allow me to get a driver's permit. While I was sitting in the classroom, I saw a king of hearts playing card tacked to the bulletin board. It disturbed me because I realized that whoever placed the card on my porch also placed one on the classroom bulletin board. He knew where I was, and that meant it could be a stalker. As I left the classroom, I took it home with me. I showed my mom, and she was a little concerned also. That very afternoon, I went outside to lie in the sun. I always lay behind our picnic table in the backyard so no one could see me. While lying on my belly, I saw another king of hearts card dangling from the bottom of the picnic table. That really scared me. The next morning, when I looked out my bedroom window, I saw a card tacked to the window screens of my bedroom. That is how it all started.

"Everywhere I went, I would find these cards, but I had no idea who was doing this or why. All I did know was that it had to be a stalker. The final straw that made my mom take me to the police was when I came home from school one day. It was Christmastime, and I had rushed home to watch *American Bandstand* on TV. I looked at the Christmas tree and saw a king of hearts card hanging there like an ornament. That meant that somehow the stalker had been in our house. I was really scared now.

"I took all these cards with me to the police. All in all there was a box full by that time. I could tell that the police detective that talked with us was concerned. He then asked me a series of questions related to school. He asked me if I knew Jim Donald. I said yes. He was a boy in my class, and he had taken me to the freshmen dance last year. The police detective then told me that his hit-and-run case that killed him was a mystery because a king of hearts card like mine was found on Jim's body. He next asked me if I knew Steve Johnson. I told the detective that I had had a few dates with him.

"The detective told me that he had been found beaten to death, and a king of hearts playing card was found lying on his beaten body. Until then the king of hearts cards were a mystery. The detective felt certain that these murders were tied to me. I realized at that point that this stalker was also a murderer. The detective then instructed me to start writing down where and when I get each king of hearts card. He said he would be checking in with me and would follow me from time to time to try and see if they could catch the stalker and thus also catch the murder. He then asked me if I was dating anyone at the present, and I told him yes. He asked me to name the boy, and they would be watching him for his safety."

Angelina continues telling Adam her story. "The stalker killed seven boys until he was finally caught in 1966. Some of these guys were just friends. I didn't date much for fear that more guys would be murdered. I had to drop out of nursing school for a year because of the notoriety and the trial of John Noble, the murderer and stalker. He went to prison for life without the possibility of parole. I thought I was finally free when he went to prison but soon found out that he could still stalk me from prison. I continue to get king of hearts cards like that one to this day. Angelina pointed to the card on the coffee table. I have a new stalker who reports my comings and goings to John Noble. He writes me threatening letters and sends me cards reporting on what he knows about me. That is why I haven't dated anyone all these years since the trial.

"I have lived in fear since 1963, and I guess I will live in fear all the rest of my life. I am now afraid for you. That is why I learned karate, and why I have two dead-bolt locks on my door. I don't ever go out alone at night, and that is why I have a fifty-dollar bill on the table beside my door. So that is my story. Everyone in Cape Girardeau knows my story, and now you know it too."

As Angelina started to cry, Adam pulled Angelina into his arms. She rested her head on his shoulder. "Don't cry, Angelina. Don't worry about me. I can take care of myself. This won't scare me off from seeing you. As I said before, I will take care of you." Adam then kissed Angelina, saying, "You are beautiful, and I can see why men want to stalk you."

Angelina felt safe in Adam's arms, and she fell asleep after the exhaustion of telling Adam her story.

Chapter Ten

The First Goodbye

Angelina gradually opened her eyes. The room was dimly lit. Her eyes focused on the man sitting across the room from her. He was smiling at her. Angelina was stretched out on Adam's couch. She was covered in a blanket.

"Did you have a nice nap?" Adam asked.

"Yes. How long have I been sleeping? What time is it?"

Adam said, "For about an hour. It is about five o'clock."

"Oh my. I'm sorry," said Angelina as she sat up.

"Don't be sorry. I've enjoyed watching you sleep. You are even beautiful when you sleep. I'm happy you felt comfortable enough to fall asleep here. I hope you're hungry. I ordered a pizza to be delivered. It should be here in about fifteen minutes."

"That sounds good. May I use your bathroom, Adam?"

"Of course, it's right down the hall on your left."

Angelina took her purse and walked down the hall. She looked at herself in the mirror. Her hair was a mess. She took her comb to straighten it and put on some lipstick. When she left the bathroom, she saw the rest of Adam's apartment and thought it was beautiful.

"Lipstick? You'll just lose it when you eat or when I kiss you," Adam said jokingly.

"Well, that is what women do. Adam, I want to apologize for crying and falling asleep like that."

"Telling your story had to be stressful. I understand. I'm just happy that you could tell me your story."

"It has been a long time since I told the story to anyone. I try not to think about it because it does stress me out. Anyway, most people who live in Cape know me and my story. I think that is why I try to isolate myself from people."

Just then the doorbell rang. Adam opened the door and paid the delivery man. He closed the door and said, "It's pizza time. What would you like to drink, Angelina?"

Angelina followed Adam to the kitchen. "Water or a Coke would be fine."

Adam got out a couple of plates.

Angelina started to sit down at the table when Adam said, "Let's eat in the living room, where it is more comfortable."

As they started to eat the pizza, Adam said, "You know that I am leaving to go back to New York in the morning."

"I wish you didn't have to go, but you told me you were just here for the weekend. I have had a wonderful time getting to know you."

"I hate to leave you also, but I will be back in a couple of weeks. I want to see you then. I will call you this week, and we can talk."

Angelina finished her slice of pizza and leaned back on the couch, saying, "That pizza was good. I have never had Pagliai's Pizza before."

"It has the reputation of being the best pizza in Cape. Aren't you going to eat more?"

"No, I am full."

"Well, I can't eat it all, so you'll have to take it home, or I'll have to throw it away." Adam smiled at Angelina and said, "I told you the lipstick was a waste of time."

Adam took Angelina home, and as they stood on the porch of her apartment, Adam grasped Angelina in an embrace and kissed her. If he had not been holding onto her, her knees would have buckled. She had never been kissed like that before. Angelina didn't want to leave his embrace but knew she had to. Adam opened her door and went in with her to turn on the lights and check all the rooms for safety. When he came back, he said, "I am going to miss you. I will be checking on you."

Adam kissed Angelia again and then was gone. Angelina sank down on her sofa and suddenly felt lonely again. She realized that she really liked Adam Harris and wanted to spend more time with him. She felt safe and secure with him and knew he was about to capture her heart. Just then the phone rang.

Angelina answered the phone, and a man's voice on the other end of the line said, "Angelina, what do you think you are doing? You are playing with fire again. You know you are mine, and I will not have you seeing another man."

"Leave me alone! You do not own me! You are in prison where you belong, and I hope you rot there!" shouted Angelina as she slammed the receiver down.

Chapter Eleven

Angelina Blooms

The night that Angelina said goodbye to Adam was a restless night. Even though she had to go to work the next morning, sleep seemed to elude her. She had a lot on her mind. She was frustrated that John Noble seemed to know her every move. She was also frightened by his threats. Should she tell Adam about his threats? She shivered, thinking about the possibility of Adam being hurt. Surely the King of Hearts stalker would not do John Noble's bidding. Nonetheless, she felt the need to tell Adam when he called her.

She smiled when she thought about Adam. He was so very handsome. She was really attracted to him like she had never been with any other man. She closed her eyes and remembered their last kiss. It was so good. It had been such a long time since she had been kissed back in 1966. The kisses from those high school boys were so long ago and really did nothing for her. She wondered if Adam could sense her inexperience.

Angelina awoke the next morning and got ready for work. She knew Adam would be leaving for New York that morning. She was going to miss him and looked forward to getting a call from him this week. At work that day, she could sense that the other employees on the floor knew she had a date that weekend. Angelina wondered what they were saying. One of the nurse assistants commented to Angelina that she appeared happy. Angelina knew she was fishing for Angelina to comment on her weekend. Angelina did not bite.

"It was a beautiful weekend. It snowed Friday night, and Saturday the weather was beautiful. I love the snow."

"Did you do anything special?" the nurse assistant continued fishing.

Damn, Angelina thought. What was she going to say now?

"I had some fun with some friends," Angelina replied as she went into the report from the night nurse.

Dr. Alan Spindler came into the unit to see his patients later in the morning. "Good morning, Ms. Harper. My wife and I really enjoyed your company Friday night. Did Adam take good care of you?"

"Yes, he did." Angelina blushed. She knew the nurse assistants were listening in on their conversation. "I want to thank you again for the invitation."

Dr. Spindler stopped talking once he saw all the nurse assistants gathering around them like vultures. He then started asking questions about his patients.

The rest of the day was busy but noneventful. At lunch Angelina was self-conscious because she knew other employees at the hospital were talking about her and her date. A person can't do anything without it turning into gossip and spreading like wildfire. Angelina wasn't sure she liked the attention. Angelina was glad to get off work that day and go home. It was exhausting to keep her guard up all day with the relentless questions from other employees and doctors. Angelina took a nap when she got home. She hardly ever did that.

On Tuesday, after work, Angelina decided to go shopping for some new clothes. She had not bought anything new in a long time because she hardly ever went anywhere special. If Adam did call her again, she wanted to be prepared to look nice for him. She had been thinking a lot about Adam and hoped she would get to see him again. She bought a couple of dresses and a new slacks outfit. She would shop for some new shoes later in the week.

Angelina arrived home about 6:00 p.m. It was just getting dark. At her apartment door was a bouquet of flowers in a vase. The only problem was that they had been torn to shreds. Angelina knew they were from Adam, but there was no card. The King of Hearts stalker had been there and had probably taken the card and destroyed her flowers. Angelina cried as she went into the apartment. "I can't have anything nice in my life without the King of Hearts spoiling everything," She knew she needed to clean up the mess, but it was getting dark outside. Instead, Angelina took the tags off her knew clothes and hung them away in her closet. At least Adam thought enough of her to send her flowers. She had never received flowers before.

Later that evening, the phone rang. Angelina was hesitant to answer it, but maybe it was Adam.

"Hello."

"Angelina? This is Adam. How are you, beautiful? I tried to call you earlier, but you must have been out. I was a little worried."

"Oh, I am fine. I went shopping after work before it got dark."

"Did you get my flowers?"

"I knew they must have been from you. They were at my front door when I got home, but I have to tell you your card was gone and the flowers were torn to shreds. It must have been the work of my favorite stalker, but thank you for being so thoughtful anyway," said Angelina.

"Damn! I should have asked the florist not to leave them if you weren't home. I am going to send you a new bouquet. When is your day off this week?"

"I am off tomorrow, but you don't need to spend the money to send me more flowers. It is the thought that counts."

"Nonsense. This makes me angry. You deserve flowers each and every day, and I'm just the man to do it."

Angelina and Adam talked quite a while that night. Her spirits were lifted. The next day she got the most beautiful bouquet of roses. The card read, "To my beautiful sunshine, who really deserves flowers each and every day."

Chapter Twelve

Angelina's Happiness

Angelina's week passed rather quickly as she awaited Adam's return to Cape Girardeau. She could hardly wait to see him again. Adam had promised that they were going to do something special but would not tell her anything more except to say she needed to dress up Friday night. As she drove home from work, she thought about the dress she was going to wear for Adam. It was emerald in color to match her eyes. When she arrived at her apartment, she found a bouquet of black roses. She became frightened and looked round to see if anyone was around. She bent down and grabbed the attached card and rushed inside her apartment. Those ugly flowers had to be from her king of hearts stalker.

She opened the card. It read,

> Angelina,
>
> I am warning you to stop playing these dangerous games with me. Don't continue to see this man. You are playing with fire.
>
> John Noble

Angelina threw the card down on the table beside the sofa and started to cry. "Will I ever be able to have happiness in my life? I hate this man. I wish he was dead."

Angelina sat up on the couch and wiped her tears away. She said, "I cannot let this ruin my weekend with Adam." She got up and started to get ready to see Adam. He was picking her up at six thirty.

After she was done, she looked at herself in the mirror and smiled. She thought she looked nice in her new dress. As she put her things in her matching new purse the doorbell rang. She looked at her watch and knew it was Adam. She almost ran to the door in excitement. As she opened the door for Adam, he came in and pulled her body to him and kissed her passionately, saying, "Angelina, I have missed you."

"I've missed you too."

"Now, where did those ugly flowers come from? Let me guess, your friendly stalker."

"Yes," said Angelina, pointing to the card on the end table.

Adam read it and wadded it up in his hand. "You're right. This is a crazy man. This is going to stop, and I'm just the man to stop him if it is the last thing I ever do. I don't want you to let this worry you this weekend. I am here to see you, and no one is going to stop me." With that, Adam opened the door, saying, "I will be back."

Adam picked up the black roses and said, "Jim, take this and throw them in the dumpster, where they'll never see the light of day. Then come back here because I want you to meet Angelina."

Angelina asked what was going on. Adam smiled and kissed Angelina's forehead. When Jim returned, Adam introduced Jim to Angelina. "Jim is my chauffeur and bodyguard. He has been with me for many years. He is going to drive wherever we go this weekend. In that way, we can talk as he takes us to our romantic destinations," Adam said smiling.

"It's nice to meet you, Jim. I'm sure you could tell me all of Adam's secrets."

"No, ma'am, if I want to keep my job," Jim said smiling.

"Well, let's roll before I get into trouble." Adam grabbed Angelina's coat, and they left the apartment. Adam took Angelina's keys and made sure the door was locked securely.

Angelina gasped as they walked to Adam's car. It was a limousine. Jim opened the door for Adam and Angelina to get in the back seat. There was a glass panel dividing the driver from the passengers.

"Is this your car also?" Angelina asked.

"Yes, Angelina. I sometimes I have to take my clients out when I am in town. They aren't as beautiful as you. By the way, I like your dress. It matches you beautiful green eyes."

"Thank you, Adam. Can I ask where you're taking me?"

Adam took Angelina's hand in his and said, "That is my secret. We will be there soon."

Jim pulled the car up in front of the New Orleans restaurant. He got out, went around the car, and opened the door so that Angelina and Adam could get out.

"We have arrived at our destination, my princess," Adam said as he took Angelina's hand to guide her to the restaurant's door. When they entered, they were met by the maître d'.

"Good evening, Mr. Harris. It's good to see you again. Let me show you to your table," he said.

He led them to the back of the restaurant. It was in a cozy corner table.

Adam took Angelina's coat and handed it off to the waiter who pulled Angelina's chair out for her to sit down. As he left, he asked Adam if he wanted his favorite wine.

"Yes, please."

"Adam, they all seem to know you here," said Angelina

"Yes, this is my favorite restaurant in Cape Girardeau. I hope you like it. Have you ever eaten here before, Angelina?"

"No, I haven't."

"Good. You are in for a treat. I wanted to take you to a place you have never been to before. I understand it is the oldest restaurant in town, and it has a lot of history."

Angelina looked around the restaurant and the people eating there. They seemed to be staring at them. Adam noticed them also.

"A lot of these people know me," he said. "The others are staring at the beautiful woman I am with. Don't be surprised if some of them don't come to the table to talk with us out of curiosity."

"Have you brought other girlfriends here before me?" Angelina asked.

"No, never."

"The only thing I remember about this restaurant was from when I was a little girl. It was a bicentennial celebration in Cape. Everyone dressed up in vintage clothing. My mom and dad drove by this restaurant, and on the balcony outside were standing five or six dancing girls in different-colored dresses."

"I remember that too. I was here in Cape Girardeau with my mother. She had been active in the historical society back then."

The waiter served Angelina and Adam supper. It was delicious. During supper a couple stopped by their table on their way out. Adam introduced Angelina to them. They were introduced as the Olivers. Mr. Oliver was a local well-known attorney. He made some kind of comment about remembering Angelina's case a few years back. He was very cordial though.

After supper, Adam and Angelina left. Jim was right there in front of the restaurant, waiting for them.

"Our evening is not over yet. There is a dance at the local Elk's Club. Do you like to dance, Angelina?"

"I did when I was in high school, so I'm sure I am rusty and don't know the recent steps."

"I will teach you what you need to know," Adam said.

Angelina had a wonderful time dancing with Adam. She felt so warm and safe in his arms. Adam whispered in her ear, "I think I am falling for you, Angelina." He then bent down and kissed the nape of her neck. Angelina felt warm all over. Adam was so handsome. She knew she was falling for him too.

When it was almost midnight Adam and Angelina left the Elks and started for home. Their evening was almost over. When they arrived at her apartment, Adam got out with Angelina. As they approached the apartment, Angelina gasped. There was red paint splashed all over her door and the word 'Harlot' was written in large letters on it.

Tears were running down Angelina's face as Adam pulled her into his arms. He motioned for Jim to come to the apartment. He handed Jim Angelina's keys to unlock the door. Jim went in first with his gun drawn. He searched the apartment to make certain it was safe. Adam led Angelina to her coach. "I have had enough of this! I am calling the police about this harassment and vandalism," said Adam.

Adam picked up the phone and dialed the Cape Girardeau Police Department. Adam said, "Yes, this is Adam Harris. I need to speak to Detective Carl Johnson. I want the police to come to my girlfriend's apartment. It has been vandalized, and she is being harassed." Adam gave the police Angelina's address. After Adam hung up, the phone immediately rang. "Let me answer it."

Adam picked up the receiver and said, "Hello." After a few seconds, Angelina heard Adam say, "You listen here, you bastard. I have called the police. If you think that I'm going to allow this crap to continue, you are sorely mistaken. You have picked the wrong man to fool with!" Adam said as he slammed down the receiver.

Chapter Thirteen

Police get involved

Jim remained outside the apartment door until the police arrived. He let the police in, and they saw Adam cradling Angelina in his arms. The police said that Detective Carl Johnson was on his way. "Ms. Harper, are you OK?" they asked.

"I am all right. I just get so tired of this," Angelina said.

"We understand," they said.

Just then Carl Johnson was ushered in by Jim.

Carl extended his right hand to Adam and said "What happened here?" as he looked at Adam.

"Angelina and I came home from our evening out and found her apartment door vandalized, as you can see," said Adam. "You know Angelina Harper?"

"Of course. I inherited her case after the trial of John Noble. We haven't heard from you, Ms. Harper, since the trial. I thought maybe things were better for you. You're a nurse now, aren't you?"

"Yes, I work at Southeast Missouri Hospital in the ICU. I didn't call you because I thought there was little you could do. I still get letters from

John Noble. I thought I could handle that as long as he was in prison. A few times he has tried to call me. But then I started getting king of hearts playing cards again like I did when I was being stalked. Then when I started dating Adam, the stalker started doing weird things like this, and he was reporting this to John Noble in prison. It was like John Noble knew everything I was doing. John Noble's letters and calls became more frequent and threatening. For instance yesterday I received a bouquet of black roses with a card or a warning to not continue seeing Adam. Now the vandalism of my apartment door. We found it like this when we came home from our date. The stalker had to have done this for John Noble."

"Do you still have the cards and letters he has been sending? If so, I would like to have them."

"Yes, I have a whole box full. I'd be happy to get rid of them. The box is on the floor of my coat closet over there," Angelina said.

"Can anything be done about this? I'm not afraid for myself because I have Jim, but I am afraid for Angelina's safety," said Adam. "I am only here on weekends. She deserves a better life than this."

Adam, I will certainly start an investigation of this. I will get back to you on what we find."

Adam walked Detective Carl Johnson out and talked with him outside. Angelina could hear them conversing outside. Angelina overheard Adam say that he was going to look into hiring someone like Jim to watch over Angelina when he is back in New York.

When Adam returned he went and sat next to Angelina on the sofa. He put his arm around her and said, "Angelina, we can't let this interfere with our weekend together. I want to gather some things together. I want you to stay with me in my apartment the rest of the weekend."

"Oh no, Adam, I can't do that. How would that look?"

"I don't care how it looks. I am not taking no for an answer. I am not going to molest you, although it is tempting. I have an extra bedroom if that is what you are worried about. For crying out loud, we are not teenagers. Now get moving."

Adam stood up and took Angelina's hand to help her stand up. He bent down and kissed her. It was the kiss she had been anticipating all evening. She looked up at Adam and said, "I can't believe I found you."

Angelina and Adam left her apartment and went to Adam's car. Jim opened the door for them and took Angelina's bag. Angelina couldn't believe she had agreed to stay with Adam in his apartment. It was so out of character for Angelina to do something like this, but she trusted Adam with her life.

Chapter Fourteen

Angelina Awakens

Angelina and Adam stayed up late talking. She had such a good time listening to Adam tell her about his life and family. "I want you to think about coming with me to New York over Thanksgiving. You could meet my mother and my sister and her family. I think you and my sister would have a lot to talk about. Do you think you could do that?"

"I will have to check my work schedule but I would love to. I've never been to New York before. I've never flown on a plane before either."

"Well, ask off," Adam said.

Angelina laid her head on Adam's shoulder and listened to the soft music playing. Adam kissed her again. "Angelina, I think I could be falling in love with you," Adam whispered. He looked down at her and found she was asleep. She probably didn't hear what he had said because she didn't reply. Adam picked Angelina up and carried her to his bedroom. He covered her up after taking off her shoes, leaned down, and kissed her on her forehead and left her for his other bedroom. He thought about how beautiful and fragile she looked in his bed. At least she would be safe tonight.

Angelina's eyes slowly opened. It was morning, and the sun was shining through the curtains. As her eyes became focused, she made a little gasp. There in front of her stood Adam, looking into his closet wearing only a white towel. He must have just taken a shower because his dark hair was still wet. Adam turned when he heard her gasp and said, "Good morning, sleepyhead. Did you sleep well?"

Angelina said, "Yes, I did. I must have fallen asleep listening to the music. What time is it?"

"It is almost nine," Adam said as he put on a long white robe, letting the towel fall to the floor. I carried you to bed. You are light as a feather."

Adam laughed when he saw Angelina look under her covers to see what she was wearing. Adam walked over to the bed and said, "I told you that you were safe with me, although I could hardly keep my hands off of you. You looked so small in my big bed." Adam bent down and kissed Angelina lightly.

"Adam, I need to get up and take a shower if I can. I feel grungy and must look awful."

"Darling, you look beautiful in the morning. My bathroom is right in there. I'll fix us some breakfast while you are beautifying yourself." With that, Adam left Angelina alone, closing the door behind him.

Angelina thought about Adam while she was getting dressed and blushed when she thought about the romantic things he had said to her. She thought to herself that she was falling in love with him. She dreamed about Adam as she slept last night. It was a beautiful dream. She remembered how he said in her dream that he thought he could be falling in love with her. Oh, if that were only true.

Angelina left the bedroom and walked down the hall to Adam's kitchen. "Something smells awfully good in here," said Angelina. "I didn't know you could cook?"

"My grandmother taught me to cook when I was a kid and came to Cape Girardeau in the summertime. Have a seat."

Angelina saw that Adam had cooked scrambled eggs, bacon, and toast and he had poured orange juice for them. It looked delicious.

"I am famished, but you have made enough for an army. I hope you are hungry," said Angelina.

"Don't worry, it won't go to waste. I think between the two of us, it will all disappear. Have you given more thought to coming to New York with me over Thanksgiving?"

"I will if I can arrange it. I would enjoy meeting your family. I feel bad that I don't have any of my family left for you to meet," said Angelina.

"I have enough family for the two of us."

After they ate breakfast and cleaned up Adam's kitchen, they left Adam's apartment. "We'll drop off your suitcase at your apartment before we head out for the day. I thought we might take a drive in the country."

When they arrived at Angelina's apartment, Angelina noticed her door had been painted and looked like it did before the vandalism the night before. "Who painted my door, Adam?"

"Jim did this morning. The paint is most likely still wet, so be careful," Adam said as he took Angelina's keys to unlock her door. Everything looked OK inside, so Angelina breathed a sigh of relief.

"Please tell Jim thank you. I am so happy that that nasty word is gone. I have great neighbors, but I worried about what they would think when they saw my door."

Adam and Angelina left for their drive in the country. It was cold, but it was a beautiful day.

Chapter Fifteen

A Night on the Town

Adam and Angelina returned to Angelina's apartment about one o'clock from their drive. "I'm taking you home so that you will have a couple of hours to get ready for our trip to St. Louis. I am taking you to a restaurant in the city, and then we have tickets to the Fox Theatre for a play."

"Oh, Adam, that sounds so exciting. I have never been to the Fox before. What in the world should I wear? I hear people really dress up for these shows."

"Your little black dress will do nicely. I like it."

"But you've already seen it, but I don't have that many fancy dresses in my closet," said Angelina.

"We'll have to remedy that someday in the future, but for now, I love the way that dress looks on you. When you wore it on our first date I fell in love with the stunning girl wearing it." That being said, Adam gave Angelina a passionate kiss, pulling her into his arms saying, "I'm crazy about you, Angelina. I'll be back at five to pick you up."

Angelina closed the door as Adam left. It was good thing the door was there to prop Angelina up after Adam's kiss. She thought she would die if he ever stopped kissing her that way. Was this what desire was all about?

Adam returned promptly at five o'clock. When Angelina opened her door, she just about fainted. There Adam stood in a black suit that looked like a tuxedo. He was so handsome. "Are you ready, my darling? You look good enough to eat. I like your hair in that updo." He helped Angelina on with her coat, and they walked toward Adam's limo. Jim was there to open the door for them.

"I have something for you, Angelina," Adam said as he helped her take off her coat. "I brought it with me from New York." Adam then handed Angelina a present to unwrap.

"Oh, Adam, what is it?" Angelina said as she took it and began to unwrap it. When she opened the box, she saw a beautiful gold necklace and earrings to match. The stones in the dainty necklace and earrings looked like diamonds. Surely they weren't diamonds, but the box said Tiffany's. She knew the name and knew that nothing cheap came from there.

"Adam, this is beautiful. You shouldn't have done this."

"Let me help you put on the necklace," Adam said as he took the necklace from Angelina's hand.

"There you go. It is perfect," Adam said as he leaned down and kissed the nape of her neck.

Angelina put on the earrings. "Do you have a mirror in this big car? I want to see how they look."

Adam laughed as he pulled a mirror down from the car's ceiling. Angelina looked at herself and told Adam she loved his gift. "It's much too expensive though, Adam."

"Nonsense. You deserve the best, and I am just the man who can give it to you."

They arrived at the restaurant in St. Louis, and Adam escorted her in on his arm.

"Mr. Harris, It has been awhile since I last saw you. How have you been?"

"Fine, Antonio."

As they were seated, Angelina said, "You seem to know everyone, Adam."

"That is a product of my trade. I have to take a lot of clients out to supper."

"I thought it was because you've taken a lot of other girls out to supper."

"Not as many as you think." Adam grinned.

They had a delicious Italian supper and then left for the theater. Jim drove up to the front door of the Fox Theatre and let them out. Everyone was looking at them as they were helped out of the limo. Angelina took Adam's arm, and they went inside. It was like a dream as she looked at the inside of the Fox. It was so beautiful. An usher showed them to their seats. Adam held Angelina's hand throughout the play. Angelina was so excited that she could hardly watch the play.

When the play was over, Adam and Angelina exited the Fox, and Jim was waiting for them outside. Angelina put her head on Adam's shoulder and thanked him for a wonderful evening. "I really enjoyed the show, Adam."

"Me too."

They talked most of the way home. Jim got out at Angelina's apartment and they slowly walked to her door. It was as though they knew they were going to have say goodbye for the next couple of weeks. Angelina didn't want to say goodbye. She knew she was going to go back to her loneliness that, through the years, she had grown to hate. Adam unlocked her door and pulled her into his arms.

"Angelina, I don't think I can leave you tonight. I want you." Adam began to kiss her, and at one point, he must have picked her up and carried her to the couch. He lay down beside her and looked into her eyes. "Please tell me you feel the same way."

"I do feel the same way. I have never felt this way before, but you must know I have never been with a man like you before."

"I know."

"How do you know?" Angelina asked.

"A man can always tell."

Angelina then gasped as she looked into Adam's eyes. "Adam, I can see myself in your eyes."

He smiled and kissed her passionately. "That is one way that I know you are innocent and inexperienced. I'm glad you haven't been close enough to look into another man's eyes. I just want you to feel my passion for you. I think I love you."

"I know I have never felt like this before. I hope you can be patient with me and give me time to understand what I really feel for you."

"I have all the patience and time in the world," said Adam. "Just let me hold you for a while before I go. I won't get to see you for a week and a half. That is a long time to not get to kiss you. I will call you every day, but that's not the same as holding you."

Adam left about an hour later, and Angelina immediately felt her loneliness. Now all she could do was think about him and wait for his return.

Chapter Sixteen

Awaiting Adam's Return

Angelina went to work on Monday and immediately called her supervisor for an appointment. She hoped that Susan Smith would give her permission to be off work the five days she needed over Thanksgiving to go to New York City with Adam. She thought she could trust Susan Smith if she told her the truth about the trip for her not to spread it all over the hospital. The hospital grapevine already was talking about her dating a handsome attorney from New York that Dr. Spindler had fixed her up with. Every time he came on the unit and saw Angelina was on duty he would ask how things were going with Adam or if she had seen Adam lately. That would fan the gossiping all over again.

Angelina went to meet with Susan Smith after work in her office. "What can I do for you, Angelina?" Susan Smith asked.

After Angelina explained the situation to Susan Smith, her supervisor said, "I heard you were seeing Adam Harris. Dr. Spindler could not help but tell his colleagues about how he had arranged for the reclusive Angelina Harper to meet Adam Harris and got you to go on a date with him. He is very proud of his work as Cupid. Alan Spindler would never forgive me if I didn't help to perpetuate this romance that he has started."

"You don't know how much I appreciate your helping me out. I have never been to New York before, and Adam wants me to meet his family."

"Knowing Adam Harris, he must think a lot of you to put forth this invitation. He would be quite a catch for any girl."

"All I know is that he has brought me out of my shell and I like him a lot," said Angelina.

"You'll have to tell me all about your trip when you return."

Angelina left Susan Smith's office. She thought that the whole hospital must know about her and Adam. Oddly enough, she didn't care anymore. When she first started seeing Adam, she didn't like the gossiping going on about her going out with Adam.

When Angelina got home, there was a box of candy delivered to her door by a man from Super D drug store. When Angelina opened the card, she saw it was from Adam. Angelina didn't like chocolate that much, but since it was from Adam, she had to have some. When Adam called her that night, Angelina thanked him for the candy.

"I didn't send you any candy," said Adam

"The card says it's from you."

"Damn, I'm afraid your stalker sent it. You haven't eaten any of it, have you?"

"Well, I have eaten three pieces," said Angelina.

"How do you feel? It might have been laced with poison."

"I fell asleep, and I didn't wake up until the phone rang. I usually don't take any naps when I get home from work."

"Don't eat any more of it. Don't throw the candy or card away, though.

I am going to have Detective Johnson come over and pick it up to have it examined."

"Oh, Adam, you don't think that John Noble is trying to kill me, do you?"

"I don't know, but we can't take any chances," said Adam. "Tell me about the rest of your day."

"Well, I have great news. My supervisor is letting me off to make the trip to New York with you over Thanksgiving."

"That is fantastic news. I can't wait to see you. We'll have five days to be together, and I can show you New York City. You can meet my mom, my sister, and her family, and you can see where I live."

"Adam, can you hold on for a minute. I think I am going to be sick."

Angelina put the receiver down and rushed to the bathroom, where she threw up and then passed out.

"Angelina! Angelina! Are you OK?" Adam hung up and immediately called the police department and paramedics in Cape. They had to break down Angelina's door. When they entered the apartment, they found Angelina lying on the bathroom floor unconscious. She was rushed to the hospital.

Carl Johnson called Adam and told him she was taken to the hospital and was unconscious.

"Carl, be sure to take that card and the candy that she ate thinking it was from me. Also, I want to make certain that her apartment is secured before you all leave."

"Don't worry, Adam. Everything will be handled. I'll call you back as soon as we find out about Angelina's condition."

Chapter Seventeen

Waiting to Hear

Adam was pacing the floor, waiting to hear from Carl Johnson about Angelina's condition. He decided to call Alan Spindler to have him check on her at the hospital. He asked Alan to give him a call back as soon as he knew something. After he hung up from Alan, he continued to pace. He wished he was in Cape Girardeau to handle things. He decided at that moment he was going to have Jim find a retired bodyguard to take care of Angelina while he was gone from Cape. He called Jim. He explained the situation to Jim and said, "I want you to hire someone like yourself to protect and do the same kinds of things that you do for me. Angelina obviously needs protection. There is a crazy man in Cape Girardeau meaning to do her harm and the bidding of John Noble, the King of Hearts. He informs John Noble about everything that Angelina does. He has got to be stopped. Do you know of anyone who might be willing to do this kind of thing for me?"

"I have a few ideas," said Jim. "I'll get on it."

"I will want to meet them, of course, and I will be the person paying them."

Just then, the phone rang, and it was Alan Spindler. "I've gone to the hospital to check on Angelina's condition. She has woken up but is very groggy. Carl Johnson says she was definitely poisoned. She has been put in a room for observation. It appears she hit her head when she fell, so they want to keep an eye on that overnight."

"Thanks, Alan. I appreciate your doing this for me."

When Carl Johnson called, he told Adam that they had replaced the door on Angelina's apartment and put two sturdy dead-bolt locks back on just like the ones she had before. "Let me tell you, it was like trying to get into Fort Knox. We had no choice but to break the door down. Once she is in that apartment, she is pretty safe."

"I thought so too, but this stalker knows my name and fooled Angelina by signing my name to the card when the candy was delivered. He obviously wants to kill Angelina."

"It has elevated this case to attempted murder, Adam. In the morning we will look into who might have bought this candy at Super D pharmacy and had it delivered. Maybe someone there will remember something. I'll let you know what we find out. In the meantime, we have posted a police officer outside her door as a precaution while she is here in the hospital."

"I have Jim looking for a bodyguard type of person like himself who I can hire to protect Angelina when I can't be in Cape. This woman is special to me. In fact, I have fallen in love with her," said Adam.

"I figured as much. Congratulations, buddy. She's a lucky woman. By the way, the news media has gotten a hold of this because she is the famous Angelina Harper. There are reporters camped out in the hospital lobby, waiting to pounce once Angelina is released from the hospital. Maybe the doctors will keep her here a few days."

"I will have to talk to the hospital's administration about doing that tomorrow morning. I will also let them know that I will pay for anything her insurance doesn't pay for. Thanks, Carl."

Adam next called the hospital and asked to be connected to Angelina's room.

"Hello," said Angelina.

"Angelina, darling, are you OK? I have been beside myself with worry. How do you feel?"

"I am tired but feeling all right otherwise. My head hurts a little. I'm sorry that I left you hanging on the phone. I wanted so much to talk to you. I'm glad I was talking to you though, because otherwise I might not have made it, they tell me."

"I love you, Angelina. I wish I was there with you. I will let you go for tonight and will talk with you again tomorrow, darling. You need some rest. Carl Johnson is on this case, and Alan Spindler is also overseeing your care. They are keeping me informed."

"Adam, I am so sorry to cause all this trouble. I don't know what I would do without you. I don't know why you love me, but I am happy you do. I love you too."

"Good night, my love."

After they hung up, Angelina thought she was the luckiest girl in the world. Adam just said he loved her. She smiled when she thought about Adam and wished he was there with her. She then realized that she would be seeing Adam in just one week. She could hardly wait. Angelina then drifted off to sleep.

Chapter Eighteen

Adam's Return

After Adam hung up the phone, he called Jim in to see him. "Jim, I have just made a decision to go back to Cape Girardeau to be with Angelina and to take care of a few things. Would you call and get you and me airline tickets? We will be staying until next Wednesday. I have two tickets already to return to New York with Angelina the following Wednesday. You will just need to get a return ticket for yourself. I feel I may need your protection for Angelina when she gets dismissed from the hospital. I understand the media in Cape Girardeau is in a frenzy because of this. They all remember the Angelina Harper and the King of Hearts story from ten years ago."

"Yes, sir. This girl is pretty important to you, isn't she? I have never seen you like this before over any woman," said Jim.

"That you haven't. This one has got a lasting grip on me, I'm afraid," Adam replied with a smile on his face. "Your job has just doubled."

The next morning Adam called his partner in the law firm and told him where he was going. He packed for the trip and met Jim at the car for their trip to the airport. During the ride Adam told Jim Angelina's story and what had been happening to her. "We have got to catch this lunatic somehow. He is trying to kill the woman I love, and we can't let that happen."

Adam and Jim landed in St. Louis and grabbed a rental car for the trip to Cape. When they arrived, Adam had Jim take him immediately to the hospital. He told Jim to take their things to the apartment and for him to get rid of the rental car. "I will call you when I am ready to leave the hospital. I want to stay with Angelina awhile, talk to Alan Spindler about Angelina's condition, and get a report from Carl Johnson."

Adam went to the nurse's station on the floor where Angelina was staying. She told Adam that she had been falling in and out of sleep, and Dr. Spindler had rescheduled a CAT scan to follow up on Angelina's concussion. She next showed where Angelina's room was. There was a police officer stationed outside. "Good afternoon, Mr. Harris," he whispered as Adam quietly entered the room.

Angelina was sleeping, and the lights were low. Adam quietly pulled a chair up to her bed. He waited for her to awaken. She was restless, he thought to himself. He gently took her fragile hand in his. She gradually opened her eyes. Immediately a big smile came over her face, and she whispered, "Adam, I can't believe you are here."

Adam stood up and leaned over Angelina's bed to kiss her. "I couldn't stay away. I have been beside myself and knew I had to come and be with you. How are you feeling, darling? I have been so worried."

"I have a headache from hitting my head in the fall. I have also been weak and sleeping an awful lot. Dr. Spindler says that is from the poison wearing off. Did you know they have police officer stationed outside my door? Why is that?"

"Angelina, they have done that at my request since this guy tried to kill you. The news media is also camped out here at the hospital trying to get to you. I asked that no one but the staff be allowed into your room. You need your rest and need to be left alone."

Angelina frowned. "This is starting all over again like it did ten years ago. You don't need this in your life, Adam. I wouldn't blame you if you said goodbye to me." Tears welled up in her eyes.

"Angelina, darling, you aren't going to get rid of me that easily. You forget, I love you."

"I am so lucky you are in my life."

Just then the door opened, and in walked Alan Spindler. He and Adam shook hands. "How is my favorite patient?" Alan Spindler asked. He looked at her head. He showed Adam the lump on Angelina's head. "I been concerned about her headaches and weakness, so I ordered a repeat CAT scan. The weakness could be just the late effects of the poison wearing off. All in all, she is really doing pretty well."

Adam asked when she might get to go home.

Alan Spindler said that if the test turned out OK she could possibly be discharged tomorrow. "I will only discharge her to your care though, Adam." Alan winked at them.

"You don't have to worry about that, Alan. I won't let her out of my sight."

After Dr. Spindler left, Angelina drifted off to sleep again. Adam called Carl Johnson to find out if there was any news about the candy and where it came from. He also wanted to let Carl know he was in Cape and was with Angelina.

Carl told Adam they had tried to follow up on the candy that appeared to be bought at Super D Drug Store. "No one remembers selling the candy, and they don't have delivery. It appears that maybe Angelina's stalker may have delivered it himself. Angelina may be able to provide us with a description. When do you think I will able to talk with her, Adam?"

"Maybe tomorrow after she is dismissed from the hospital."

Chapter Nineteen

Angelina's Desire

The next day, Angelina was dismissed from the hospital. Adam had arranged with Jim to come and pick them up in the Mercedes. He instructed Jim to not get out of the car and to keep it running since the hospital staff would bring her out to the car in a wheelchair. Adam knew the news media would try to talk to Angelina if they were alerted to her discharge. As soon as they were in the car, Jim could drive off. Jim was to take them to Adam's apartment.

"Why are we going to your apartment, Adam?" Angelina asked.

"It is safer there because Jim will be with us. Also, the news media will think we are going to your apartment and will head there. I want to fool them. There is no way that they can get near my apartment."

Angelina knew that was true. Her apartment door was exposed to the outside. The only way anyone could get to Adam's door was through the iron gate of his garage that closed and locked behind the car once it entered the garage. His apartment entrance was only accessible through the garage. Jim's apartment was right below Adam's apartment.

"But, Adam, I have none of my clothes or other things that I need. I won't have my cosmetics."

"I promise, we will go to your apartment tomorrow and get everything you think you need. In the meantime, you can wear what they brought you to the hospital in or this fluffy robe that I bought you," Adam said with a grin.

"It is beautiful, I will admit, but that is not what I had in mind."

Jim next drove into Adam's garage without any reporters trying to follow him. When they got out of the car, Jim grabbed Angelina's things from the hospital, and Adam picked Angelina up to carry her up to his apartment.

"Adam, I can walk. I'm not helpless."

"You heard Alan say you are to stay off steps for now since you are still wobbly. I am just following the doctor's order, so hush."

When they got to Adam's apartment, Jim unlocked the door, turned off the alarm, and put Angelina's things down. "Is there anything else I can get for you, sir?" Jim asked.

"No, but thanks, Jim."

Adam carried Angelina to his couch and sat her down as Jim left. "How do you feel sitting up, darling?"

"I'm fine. I just still have a bit of a headache. I'll be glad when that goes away."

"Jim has your prescriptions to get filled. He will be getting those soon. I understand it is something you can take safely for your headache," said Adam.

Adam went to his refrigerator to get something to drink. "Angelina, do you want a Pepsi or something else to drink?"

"A Pepsi would be great. How did you remember that I love Pepsi?"

"I remember everything about you, sweetie." Adam grinned as he went to sit with Angelina on the couch. He could hardly wait to take her in his arms and kiss her. "You are so beautiful, Angelina. I can't keep my hands off you." He then kissed her passionately.

Angelina trembled. "I've missed you so much. I don't know what I would have done without you." Angelina put her head on his shoulder as he continued to kiss her.

"Angelina, please say you are mine. Please surrender to me. I don't know how much longer I can be satisfied with just kissing you."

"Adam, you need to give me some time. You know I want you too, but I have never been with a man like you." Angelina put her hand on Adam's chest and started fingering a button on his shirt.

Adam looked at what Angelina was doing and grasped her hand as his breath caught in the back of his throat. "Angelina, you tell me no, but your actions say yes. You are playing with fire."

"Can you just hold me for now, Adam? I just don't know what is happening to me."

"It is called desire, Angelina," said Adam as he gathered her into his arms.

Just then there was a knock at Adam's door. "It must be Jim with your medicine."

Angelina sat up and adjusted the robe around her legs. Adam took the medicine from Jim and came back to the couch. He read the label on the bottle, took one of the capsules out of the bottle, and handed it to Angelina, saying, "This will make you sleepy, but it is intended to help your headache."

After Angelina swallowed the pill, Adam picked her up and carried her to his bedroom. He laid her in his king-size bed and covered her up. "You look so tiny in my big bed."

"Adam, will you stay with me until I go to sleep?"

Adam lay down beside Angelina on top of the covers and kissed her forehead. Angelina gradually drifted off to sleep. When Angelina awakened, she found Adam asleep beside her. It was close to dusk. They must have slept for several hours.

Angelina started to get up. Adam said, "Where are you going, darling?"

Angelina said she was going to the bathroom.

"Then come right back to me. I want to talk to you."

Angelina crawled back into bed, and Adam turned on his side to face Angelina. "I never answered you when you asked me to give you some time. I will be content for now to give you time to adjust to my desire. When you feel uncomfortable, just say no to me. But remember, I am a man who loves you very much. I hope you know that this is not just a passing fling. I want you in my life forever."

"I feel the same way, Adam. I guess I have heard too many stories about girls falling in love and then the guy leaves them after they get what they want."

Adam laughed. "Horny teenage boys do that, but when you get to my age, you don't say 'I love you' easily. Men won't say that unless they really mean it. Saying I love you is a commitment that is hard to say. I am committed to you, Angelina."

"I am also afraid of getting pregnant. Adam, I am not on the pill."

"I understand, but real men know how to handle that too. I am not inexperienced, Angelina. Besides, if I am an honest man and committed to you, I would never leave you if you became pregnant. That would give me an excuse to marry you." Adam laughed and winked at Angelina. "Now I don't know about you, but I am starving. Let me call Jim and have him go out and pick us up some grub."

"That sounds wonderful."

Chapter Twenty

Surrender

Angelina and Adam ate their Chinese food that Jim had for them. They then sat on the sofa for hours, talking about their upcoming Thanksgiving trip to New York City. Then the phone rang, and Adam got up to answer it.

"Hello," said Adam. "She's not here." There was a long pause as Adam listened. "You listen to me, you son of a bitch. This has gone on long enough. I warn you to stop harassing Angelina. You can threaten all you want, but you are threatening the wrong man. I assure you that you'll will be caught, and if I ever catch you, you are a dead man," said Adam as he slammed the receiver down.

Adam then picked up the phone to alert Jim to the threatening call he received.

"Was that my King of Hearts' stalker?" asked Angelina. She was trembling, with tears rolling down her face. "How did he find out who you are?"

"This guy is a maniac. He threatened me, trying to get me to take you home. He is nuts."

Adam gathered Angelina in his arms and held her. "Now I want you to stop crying. Where is that brave young woman that I love? I've always told you that I am here to take care of you, and that is what I am doing. Nothing is going to happen to us, I promise you."

Adam picked Angelina up, and carried her to bed. "It is midnight and you need to get some sleep. Tomorrow we have a big day because we need to go over to your apartment and get your things. Jim will help us collect your things."

"Adam, would you sleep beside me tonight? I don't think I can sleep after that call. I just need you near."

"That is something I could never say no to." Adam lay down on the bed and gathered Angelina close to him. "Just don't start playing with my button again."

"Oh, Adam, I feel so warm and safe with you. I love you more than I ever thought I could love any man."

"Then surrender to me, Angelina. I love you and want you too."

Angelina relaxed, and Adam undid her furry robe. He touched Angelina's bare skin beneath the robe. His breath caught, and he mumbled that she was so beautiful and she belonged to him. Angelina put her arms around Adam's neck and gave herself to Adam at that moment. Angelina felt as though she was in heaven. She could not control her body's desire for him. She did not have the strength to even try and say no. It was the most desire she had ever experienced, and she did not want it to end.

Adam kept holding Angelina after he stopped. "I did not hurt you did I, Angelina? I just love you so much that I couldn't stop myself."

Angelina held on to Adam. "You didn't hurt me. It was beautiful. I never imagined that having sex was such a beautiful thing. I wish I had met you years ago. You are my one true love. I just wanted you so much too. I couldn't stop, and I knew I had to surrender to you or die."

Adam kissed Angelina passionately. He then picked up her naked body and carried her to his Jacuzzi. They bathed together. "You have a beautiful body, Angelina. You take my breath away just as you did the first time I laid eyes on you at the hospital. I made Alan introduce me to you. I asked Alan who that stunningly beautiful woman was. I said 'I must meet her.' That's when he told me you had a story but he would introduce me. That's when I knew I couldn't resist you. The rest is now history. I've now fallen hopelessly in love with you."

"Have you ever felt this way with any other women, Adam? You are so handsome there must have been plenty of other women in your life."

"There has never been anyone like you. I've had my share of women throw themselves at me, but they had artificial beauty. I never loved any of them the way I love you. Please believe me."

"Do you still see any of them?"

Adam replied, "No, I don't date any of them anymore. I see some of them around from time to time, but no dates with any of them. They don't hold a candle to you."

Adam stood up in the Jacuzzi and grabbed a big fluffy towel to wrap around himself. Angelina gasped as she looked at his naked body. *Could he really be mine?* she asked herself.

Adam bent down and helped Angelina stand before him. He took another big towel and dried her off before wrapping it around her. He next carried her to bed and took her towel from around her body and told her to get into bed. He dropped his towel and climbed into bed with her. "Now we sleep," he said as he cradled her in his arms.

It was so warm and cozy in Adam's bed and in his arms that she went to sleep easily.

The next morning when they awoke, Adam made love to her again. It was just as passionate as it was the first time. She knew she was such a lucky woman to have a man want her like Adam did. It was such blissful surrender.

Chapter Twenty-One

Vandalism

Angelina and Adam went over to her apartment to collect her things not only for the next few days but also for the trip to New York City. Jim drove them so he could help. When they arrived and Adam opened the door to Angelina's apartment so they could go in, Adam stopped her before they entered. The apartment had been ransacked. Everything was destroyed. Nothing was in its place. Adam motioned for Jim to go into the apartment first. Jim drew his gun and entered to make certain that no one was still there.

"Adam, how did he get into my apartment?"

"I don't know, but we are going to find out. Jim is looking around. I need to call the police. Your fifty dollars by the door is gone. You didn't need that to see someone had been in here."

Adam called the police to report the intrusion. He talked to Carl Johnson, who said they would be right out. "Don't move anything until they get here, Angelina. They will want to dust for prints when they get here."

Angelina sat down on her sofa to wait for the police. Jim came to speak to Adam about what he found. "It looks like he gained entry through this front window. Come with me. I want to show you something," he said. They entered Angelina's bedroom, and there on the bed was Angelina's black party dress with a long knife through it.

"Damn," Adam said.

About that time Angelina entered the room and screamed. "My little black dress that you like so well. He means to kill me, doesn't he?"

Adam went to her side and said, "Over our dead bodies, Angelina."

"Let me take you back to the sofa, Ms. Angelina," said Jim.

Carl Johnson arrived with a couple of other officers. One started taking pictures, and the other started dusting for fingerprints. Carl Johnson said they were going to have to take her black dress and the knife along with them to keep for evidence. Angelina agreed.

"Adam, could you or Jim go and get my mail? Are my keys and purse around here somewhere?" asked Angelina.

"We will look for your purse and keys," said Adam.

"I'm glad I didn't leave you here after leaving the hospital. This place isn't as safe as you thought it was," said Adam as he handed her his handkerchief. Angelina was crying.

"I wonder if my car is OK."

"Jim, you go check on it please."

"Yes, sir."

Carl Johnson came back into the living room. "She's not planning on staying here any longer, is she?"

"No, I won't let her. We just came over to get her things so she can stay with me. She wanted her mail and to move her car to my place. I won't be letting her out of my sight. It is virtually impossible for anyone to get into my apartment. Jim is in the apartment downstairs, and he monitors the outside of the building that I own. There are only the two apartments that is in this building. Access is only gained through the iron gate that our cars enter into the secured garage. You know where I live when I am here in Cape. I am going to get an unlisted phone number tomorrow since I got a threatening call last night. So this guy knows who I am. Jim will be going with us wherever we go. This coming Wednesday, I am taking Angelina with me to New York City for Thanksgiving to meet my family," said Adam.

Jim came into the room and told Angelina her car seemed OK but he would check it closer before she drove it. He handed her a purse and keys, saying they were found in the bedroom, on the floor under some of her clothes. "I will go check on your mail."

Carl and one of the other officers left. "We've done as much as we can do at this time. I am leaving one officer outside until you pack up Angelina's things and leave. I would suggest you don't return. This obviously is not a safe place."

Jim had already started picking up the mess in Angelina's kitchen area. Angelina and Adam straightened the furniture in the living room. There was very little that Angelina wanted to take with her from the living room. Angelina went to her bathroom and collected her cosmetics and toiletries that she wanted to have with her. They next went to her bedroom to gather her clothes. Jim brought in two suitcases that Adam had brought along, knowing that Angelina probably didn't have any. What didn't fit in the suitcases, they put in large trash bags to move to Adam's place. She put her bills and other mail in a small bag along with a book she had been reading. They then left her apartment, but the news media was there wanting to question Angelina. "Please leave me alone. I have nothing to say," she said.

Jim drove around until he was certain no one was following them before going to Adam's apartment.

Chapter Twenty-Two

Getting Ready for the Trip

Jim and Adam put Angelina's things in Adam's apartment. Adam told Angelina he was going to take Jim back to the apartment so that Angelina's car could be moved to his garage. "You will be safe here for that short period of time. Don't answer the telephone though." Adam kissed Angelina on her forehead and said, "We'll only be gone a few minutes, darling."

When Adam returned he told Angelina her car had been safely moved. He sat down beside Angelina on the sofa. "Jim put all your things in my spare bedroom so that you would have a closet to hang your clothes in. Don't get any ideas that you will be sleeping in there though," Adam said with a grin. "You will be sleeping with me."

"Adam, what am I going to do for a party dress since my little black dress has been destroyed? Can I go shopping before we leave for New York?"

"You can't go by yourself. Jim and I will go with you. I know of only two nice places in Cape that my sister used to frequent for party dresses, Hecht's and Rust and Martin. I know both of the owners."

"You know everybody," Angelina joked.

The next day, Adam and Jim took Angelina shopping. She tried on dresses for Adam. He had told the clerk he wanted to see Angelina in a black dress and an emerald green dress. When Angelina came out in the green dress, Adam's said, "Wow. That dress I love, don't you, Angelina?"

"Yes, I like it too. How much is it?" Angelina asked the clerk.

"Forget about the cost. I am paying for these dresses," Adam said. "No arguing, darling."

Angelina tried on several black dresses, but Adam did not react well to any of them until the last black dress was tried on. It was sleeveless and cut just low enough in the front to show a little cleavage. "Um, that is gorgeous on you. You look good enough to eat. It shows all your beautiful curves."

Angelina blushed as she went back to the dressing room. When she came out, Adam was paying for the dresses. "Is there anything else you need for our trip? You and my sister Cathy will be going shopping the day after Thanksgiving though."

"No, Adam, I don't need another thing."

Adam thanked the clerk for her help, and they left Hecht's. Jim was waiting with the car. As they were about to get in the car, they heard a woman's voice yell out, "Angelina, Angelina, wait up!"

Angelina looked in the direction of the voice. It was a fellow nurse she worked with at the hospital.

"Hi, Sally, how are you? I miss everyone at the hospital."

"We miss you too. Introduce me to this gorgeous man you are with."

Angelina introduced Sally to Adam. They talked awhile, and then Angelina told Sally she would not be returning to work until after Thanksgiving. They said their goodbyes and then climbed into Adam's car.

"Jim looked a little nervous when we were talking to Sally," said Angelina.

"I wasn't real happy either, I must say, with that maniac lurking around."

"Oh, Adam, nothing is going to happen in broad daylight. Nothing can ruin our day out together."

"You're probably right. How about going somewhere for lunch?"

"That sounds great," said Angelina.

"Jim take us to Garfield's in the mall. They have the best fried mushrooms in town."

Angelina whispered, "Can Jim eat with us?"

"Of course. We won't be going anywhere without Jim."

As Angelina, Adam, and Jim ate their lunch, Angelina felt uneasy. Jim seemed to be looking at everyone, and everyone seemed to staring at the three of them. Angelina also felt like many of the other patrons were talking about her.

"What's the matter, Angelina? You seem a little nervous."

"Oh, I just feel like people are staring and talking about us. I guess I am reliving my former paranoid days when the King of Hearts was stalking me as a teenager."

"I'm afraid that maybe some of these people have seen your picture in the paper with the article about your poisoning," said Adam. "Just ignore them. More likely though they are talking about how beautiful you are."

Chapter Twenty-Three

The New York Trip Begins

That night Adam and Angelina made passionate love. Angelina could not believe how much she loved Adam. He was so strong and virile that she could not resist him. He always cuddled with her as they slept. That night she prayed that he would never grow tired of her.

The next morning Jim hauled in three suitcases and told Angelina that Adam had gotten them for her for the trip to New York. "You'll need these to pack today since we are leaving for New York in the morning."

"Thank you, Jim."

As Angelina was starting to pack, Adam came in and asked her to take a break because he wanted to talk to her. He led her to the living room and had her sit on his sofa. "Angelina, I have something very important to talk with you about." Angelina looked very puzzled by Adam's seriousness.

"What is it, Adam? Have I done something wrong?"

"Of course not, sweetie," Adam said. "You know I have loved you from the moment I first laid my eyes on you. I have known all along that I cannot live without you. That is why I have a big question to ask you."

Adam got down on one knee, opened a small box from his pocket, and said, "Angelina, darling, will you marry me?"

Angelina's mouth flew open. She began to tremble with joy. "Adam, you know I will. I can't believe you want me. I love you so much."

Angelina looked at the ring. It was gorgeous. Adam told her it was a five-karat emerald-shaped diamond with two baguette emeralds, one on each side of the diamond. "The emeralds are intended to match your eyes. Do you like it?"

"Oh, Adam, it is beautiful, but it is so big."

Adam slid it on Angelina's finger. "It is the perfect size for the woman of my dreams. I want everyone to know you are mine."

Angelina looked at it sparkling in the sunlight. She put her arms around Adam and gave him a kiss. "I feel as though I am living a dream. I'm glad I saved myself all these years for you."

Adam kissed her passionately. He then got up and opened a bottle of pink champagne in celebration. He called Jim to come up to the apartment to announce to him that he now had officially two people to care for. He gave Jim a glass of champagne. Jim toasted to the two of them and said, "Congratulations." Jim then left them alone.

"I have some other things to discuss with you, Angelina. I hope you won't be angry with me, but I told your landlord that you wouldn't be returning to your apartment. I paid off your lease. I also changed your address to mine so that all your mail comes here. If you have anything else you want from your apartment, Jim will go and get it. I want you to stay with me, and I never want you to be without me. Is that OK with you?"

"Yes, Adam. I feel safe here with you and don't want to ever be without you again. I love you with my whole heart."

"When we return from New York after Thanksgiving, I also want you to resign from the hospital. I am independently wealthy and have enough money to take care of you forever. Where I go, you will go. We will travel the world together, and you will have the freedom to do whatever you want. I will continue to work, but you will make new women friends. You won't be bored, I promise you. We will have a great social life in New York and Cape Girardeau."

Angelina kissed Adam a little longer, then he said, "We need to finish packing so we can have a good night's sleep before leaving for the airport in St. Louis in the morning. I can't wait to introduce you to my mother and sister along with some our other friends. My mother will be especially happy since she has been after me to settle down for years. I think she has given up on me."

After they finished packing, Angelina said, "I hope I haven't forgotten anything."

"Don't worry about it. Whatever you don't have, I will buy for you in New York."

That night after she and Adam made love, she fell asleep nestled in Adam's arms. He was so warm beside her. She couldn't imagine her life without him.

That morning she awoke to Adam kissing her and saying, "Wake up, my sleepyhead. It's time for your big trip to the big city. I have some coffee for you to help you wake up. Did you sleep well?"

"Yes, I slept like a baby. Thanks, Adam. That coffee smells so good."

As Jim drove to St. Louis, Adam and Angelina talked about the itinerary for the next few days. "Tonight we will attend a cocktail party at my mother's house. Our friends along with my sister and her family will be there. That is where I will announce our engagement. The next day, of course, is Thanksgiving at my mom's. The next day you will go shopping with my sister. You and I will have Saturday to ourselves to explore New York before coming home on Sunday."

Chapter Twenty-Four

Thanksgiving Eve

Adam and Angelina boarded the plane for New York. They had first-class seats, including Jim. Angelina whispered to Adam that she had never been on a plane before. "I'm a little nervous about this," said Angelina.

"Don't worry, darling. Just hold my hand."

The stewardess asked them to fasten their safety belts. The pilot came on the intercom and said it should be a smooth flight to New York City and they should arrive there in two hours or so. The plane engines revved up, and Adam held Angelina's hand a little tighter. After they were airborne, the stewardess came around and offered the first-class passengers something to drink. "I'll take a beer, and the lady will have a glass of wine to settle her nerves."

Angelina did not like the stewardess because she seemed to be flirting with Adam. She didn't blame her, because Adam was so handsome, but Angelina took Adam's hand as she left and said, "I think she is flirting with you."

"Don't worry, sweetie. I'm not interested. She will eventually get the hint."

Adam was right. He gave the stewardess the cold shoulder, and she backed off.

"Do you have a lot of women flirt with you?" asked Angelina.

"I have my share, especially once they think I have money. Those types of women are a dime a dozen, and they turn me off. When someone flirts with me like that, you take my hand or arm and let them know I am yours."

The plane landed in New York City just as the captain had said. It was a smooth landing. The passengers in first class were the first to exit the plane. Adam and Jim collected their luggage, and they headed to Adam's car that was parked at the airport parking lot. Angelina was in awe of the city as Jim drove them to Adam's hotel. Jim said, "I'll see to the luggage and car. The two of you go on up to the penthouse."

Angelina and Adam were greeted by the hotel manager. "Welcome home, Mr. Harris," he said. Adam introduced Angelina to him and said, "This is Angelina Harper, my fiancée."

"Welcome, Ms. Angelina. I was beginning to think Adam was a confirmed bachelor. I can see why he chose you. Enjoy your stay."

Adam and Angelina took the elevator to the top of the hotel. When they got off, Adam told the elevator operator that Jim would be following them up with their luggage. The young man said, "Yes, sir."

As Angelina entered Adam's apartment, her mouth fell open. "This is beautiful, Adam. Have you lived here long?"

"About five years. I found it was a lot easier to have a place closer to my work rather than traveling back and forth every day from my mom's house. This is perfect for me to entertain clients if I need to. Let me show you around."

Angelina went to the patio outside the living room area and marveled at the view of the New York skyline. Adam showed her some of the buildings that she might recognize including the Empire State Building. "You think this is beautiful, just wait until you see the night lights."

Adam and Angelina went downstairs to the dining room for lunch. When they returned to the apartment, they found that their luggage had been delivered, so they began to unpack. Adam opened his closet so that Angelina could hang her clothes beside his. "What should I wear tonight, Adam? The black dress or the green dress?"

"I think you would look elegant in your little black dress. You look sexy in it," he said, winking at her.

"The black one it is, then."

Angelina and Adam started getting ready for the party at his mom's house. "Do you think she will like me, Adam?"

"I know she will, darling. Don't worry about that."

Once they were dressed, Adam stood beside Angelina. He was gorgeous in his black tuxedo. She matched him perfectly in her black dress. "Look, Adam, I am wearing the diamond jewelry you got for me. I was afraid my stalker had taken it, but Jim found it for me at my old apartment."

Jim smiled to himself because he knew the stalker had taken it, but he had the set replaced so that Angelina would never know.

Just then the doorbell rang. "Don't ever answer this door if I am not here. Jim monitors the door and will let you know if it is OK to let the person in. He will accompany the person in."

Adam opened the door and said, "Hello, Pierre. I've been expecting you. Angelina, Pierre is here to show you some wraps. It is cold outside, and you need something to cover your shoulders for the trip to my mom's house."

Angelina looked at the rack of jackets. "I'm not much for mink, Adam, but I will look at the other things." Pierre helped her try on several wraps. "What do you think of this one, Adam? It not only goes with this dress, but I could wear it with the green dress as well."

It was a white furry jacket. Adam winked at Pierre, knowing that it was just as expensive as the mink stoles. "It is perfect. We will take it." Adam signed for the purchase and said goodbye to Pierre.

After Pierre left, Angelina looked at the price tag. Her mouth fell open. "Adam, this is way too expensive. It is as expensive as the mink jackets."

"That is because it is white mink. It is beautiful on you. Are you ready? We need to meet Jim at the elevator."

Adam was right. It was very cold outside as they climbed into Adam's limo. "It is about an hour's drive to Mom's house so make yourself comfortable. Do you want a glass of wine to warm yourself up?"

Angelina took a small glass of wine from Adam. "I'm not use to drinking very much. I don't want to appear tipsy when I meet your family."

"You'll be fine with this little glass."

When they arrived and the house of Adam's mom, Angelina said the house was so big and beautiful. "It is like a mansion."

"This is where I was born and raised, darling."

There were a lot of cars in the driveway. They had valet parking, and Jim took the ticket from the valet so they could retrieve the car later. Adam ushered Angelina into the foyer. It was massive, with a winding staircase and a huge chandelier. Adam helped Angelina off with her jacket and handed it and her purse to the matron. He told Angelina if she needed her handbag later, she could come and ask for it.

Adam then ushered Angelina into the large living area where all the guests were. When they entered, it got quieter in the room. Everyone was staring at them. A lovely, regal lady came over to them and gave Adam a hug. "Adam, I have been waiting to meet this young lady who seems to have captured you heart."

"Angelina, as you can guess this is my mother, Cathy Harris. Mom, this is Angelina Harper. I found Angelina in your home town of Cape Girardeau."

"It is nice to meet you, ma'am."

"Come on in and get something to drink while I go and hunt down your sister."

"Adam, I don't want any alcohol. Could you get me something that just looks like alcohol?"

"Your wish is my command, my lady."

As Adam headed to the bar area, a young woman hollered Adam's name. She ran up to him and flung her arms around him and kissed him on his lips. "Adam, what have you been doing with yourself? I have missed you so."

As Adam unwrapped himself from this woman, Angelina thought that she surely wasn't his sister. "Cindy, it's nice to see you again. Come, I want to introduce you to someone." Adam ushered this Cindy person to where Angelina was standing and introduced her as a good friend of his sister's from their old college days. Angelina said hello and then Adam ushered Angelina with him to the bar to get their drinks. Angelina met Adam's sister Carolyn, who she felt was much more refined. They talked together quite a while. Adam commented that Cindy Cramer was there and she was her usual flirtatious self.

"Well, you know Cindy has been after you for years, Adam. She doesn't seem to want to give up. I've tried to tell her that she is not your type, but she doesn't seem to want to understand," said Carolyn.

"I hope that after tonight she gets the message. I will be officially announcing that I am off the market," Adam said as he showed Carolyn Angelina's hand.

"Oh my god, Adam, I can't believe you have finally fallen in love. I was beginning to write you off as a confirmed bachelor. Have you told Mom yet?"

"No, it is to be a surprise. I'm going to announce our engagement now."

Adam took Angelina's hand and took her to the bandstand, where the orchestra was playing. He tapped on his glass to get everyone's attention. "I have an announcement to make," said Adam. "I want everyone to meet my fiancée, Angelina Harper. We are going to plan our wedding for early next year. I can't wait to make her my bride."

Everyone cheered as Adam's mom made her way to the bandstand. "Oh, Adam, I can't tell you how happy you have made this old woman. I was about to give up on you. Welcome, Angelina, to our family."

After everyone offered their congratulations and toasted to Angelina and Adam's engagement, Angelina excused herself to find the ladies' room. She got her purse and was directed upstairs. As she was returning back downstairs, a man stopped her on the staircase and said, "You are the most gorgeous woman at this party. I want to dance with you." Angelina tried to push herself away from him, but he didn't seem to take no for an answer. He was drunk, she could tell. He had his hand on her shoulder, and she tried to brush it off.

"You, sir, need to take your hands off of my woman. Who the hell are you anyway, and how did you get invited to this party?"

"I am here with Cindy Cramer."

"Well, I suggest you go find her and molest her. Better yet, I think it is time for the two of you to leave. I am sure Cindy is about as drunk as you."

The man grumbled and staggered down the steps.

"Are you OK, Angelina? I'm sorry I didn't rescue you sooner. I should have known he was Cindy's date. I'll make certain that they leave."

Adam bent down and kissed Angelina and said, "I am so proud of you. I'm surprised you didn't use your karate on him."

"I was afraid he was family, and I didn't want to make a scene."

The rest of the evening was wonderful. They danced together, and Angelina enjoyed being in Adam's arms. She always felt so safe there.

Chapter Twenty-Five

Thanksgiving

Angelina and Adam slept later on Thanksgiving morning. Angelina got up first to take a shower. She was in the shower when Adam joined her. "I couldn't resist showering with my lovely Angelina. We'll have to do this more often. I can't believe my good fortune to have such a beautiful woman in my bed and in my shower. I love you Angelina," Adam said as he bent down to kiss her.

"When do we have to leave for your mom's house, Adam?"

"We'll have to leave here about 3:00 p.m. We have plenty of time to be playful with each other." Adam turned off the shower and picked her up and carried her out of the shower and to his bed. He dried her off with a towel and then dried himself off. He lifted Angelina into the bed and made love to her.

They jumped into the hot tub for a while. When Adam got out, he helped Angelina out, and they wrapped themselves in their robes. Adam went to the living room and called for room service to deliver some breakfast even though it was almost lunchtime.

They discussed their upcoming wedding as they ate their late breakfast. "Where are we going to get married, Adam?"

"Do you want to have a ceremony in Cape, Angelina? We will, of course, have a ceremony here in New York too."

"Adam, I don't want to have a wedding ceremony in Cape Girardeau. I don't have much family in Cape anymore, and I don't want to worry about the King of Heart's stalker showing up and ruining our wedding day. I would rather get married here and just invite what little family I have."

"My mother and sister are here to help you with the planning, which will be helpful to you. When do we want to get married? Have you thought about a date?"

"No, I haven't, Adam. You told everyone last night we were going to marry after the first of the year. It takes time to plan a wedding. Maybe we should talk to your mom and sister about it today. We'll have to reserve a church and a reception hall, which might be a challenge with a short time frame."

"We will marry in my childhood church, and the reception will be held at my mother's home. She won't have it any other way. You will have to spend a lot of time here in New York for the planning, which I will be happy about," Adam said. "I don't want you to stay in Cape without me any longer."

Angelina and Adam continued to talk about their wedding plans as they dressed for Thanksgiving. "What should I wear today, Adam?"

Adam went to the closet and pulled out a peach-colored dress that Angelina usually wore to church on Sundays. "This will do nicely."

Adam called Jim to bring the limo around to the front of the hotel about 2:00 p.m. Angelina heard a noise outside the penthouse apartment on the street below. She went to the patio and looked down on the street below. "Adam, it's the Macy's Thanksgiving parade, with all the character balloons and bands. It is exciting to see the parade in person instead of having to watch it on TV like I did when I was a little girl."

Adam joined her on the balcony and said it was always a beautiful parade. "I had better tell Jim to meet us at back of the hotel. We'll never get away from here in front."

When Angelina and Adam arrived at Cathy Harris's home, they were greeted by Carolyn, her husband Jack, and their two daughters. The little girls were eleven and nine years old. They had long brown hair and were beautiful kids. They immediately asked to see Angelina's engagement ring. Their mouths fell open, and they oohed and aahed.

"Girls, don't make yourselves pests," said their mother, Carolyn.

Just then Adam's mother appeared and gave both Angelina and Adam a kiss, saying, "Happy Thanksgiving. We are all in the living room watching the Macy's Thanksgiving parade while our Thanksgiving feast is being prepared. The parade is almost over, and next we'll have football after we eat. That's usually the way our Thanksgiving goes around here."

During the meal, Angelina and Adam's wedding was discussed. Adam said Angelina would be staying in New York to plan the wedding with Cathy and Carolyn's help. He told them they were going back to Cape Girardeau on Sunday to see after things there and would be returning to New York after a couple of days. "Mom, we have decided to have the wedding at our church and would like to have the reception here at the family home, if that is OK."

"Most certainly, Adam. I wouldn't have it any other way. Angelina and I will have to put together an invitation list and pick out invitations. You need to reserve the church, Adam. Have you two set a wedding date?"

"I don't want to wait forever," said Adam. "It should be sometime after the first of the year. I think January or February at the latest would be good. Angelina, what do you think?"

"My birthday is February 29. What do you think about that date? Next year will be a leap year, and it falls on a Saturday. That would give us three months for planning. Would that work for you Adam?"

"That's great."

Everyone toasted to February 29.

Thanksgiving Day was a wonderful day. Angelina had not had a thanksgiving like this with family for so long. She realized that she missed her mom and dad and the Thanksgivings that they had had through the years. While the men excused themselves and went to the living room to watch football, the women stayed in the dining room, talking about their shopping trip tomorrow and other shopping they would have to do for the wedding once Angelina returned to New York next week.

When the women finally joined the men in the living room, they found the men shouting and hollering during the football plays. Adam asked Angelina if she would like a glass of wine, which he got for her when she said yes.

About 10:00 p.m. Adam and Angelina left for the city and Adam's apartment. "I had such a great time today getting to know your family, Adam. I am looking forward to being with them to plan the wedding and to go on our shopping trip tomorrow."

"I can tell they love you just as much as I knew they would. You belong here with me. We will have a great life together, darling. I can hardly wait until February 29, when I make you mine forever."

Chapter Twenty-Six

The Shopping Trip

Jim took Angelina and Adam to pick up Adam's sister, Carolyn, on the Friday after Thanksgiving for their shopping trip. Jim then drove Adam to his mom's house so that he could spend the day with her. She always needed Adam to help with the decoration of the family home for Christmas. The plan was that Jim would take Angelina and Carolyn shopping and then bring them back to the estate once they were tired of shopping.

"Jim, we first want to go to Maurice's. That is where I hope to find my husband's Christmas present," said Carolyn. "Angelina might find something she likes there for Adam also."

When they entered the jewelry store, Carolyn asked to look at men's watches. Angelina was drawn to the men's gold bracelets. While Angelina was looking at them, Carolyn picked out a beautiful watch for her husband. Maurice next came over and asked if he could show her something in the case.

"I'd like to look at these men's gold bracelets, if I may."

"Most certainly, mademoiselle."

As Angelina picked up the one she liked most to examine it and show it to Caroline, Maurice said, "You must be Adam Harris's fiancée?"

"How did you know? Do you know Adam Harris?"

"Most certainly. I recognized the engagement ring that Adam bought here for you. I designed it. He insisted on adding the emeralds to match your green eyes. Do you like the ring?"

Angelina replied that she loved it. She next asked Carolyn if she thought Adam would like and wear the gold bracelet.

"He would love it, Angelina. He has nothing like it."

"Do you think he would wear it, Carolyn?"

"He would most certainly wear it especially if it comes from you."

"Maurice, I will take it. Can you wrap it up for me in Christmas paper with a card from me? I will give it you, Carolyn, to make certain that it is under the Christmas tree."

Jim next took them to Macy's. Carolyn bought several gifts, including one for her mother, one for Adam, and a couple for her daughters. Angelina did the same with Carolyn's help. Angelina also bought a couple of long negligees after she tried on several.

"Adam won't be able to resist you in those, Angelina," said Carolyn.

"Let us go to Sherry's Restaurant for lunch. It was the restaurant featured in the movie, *Breakfast at Tiffany's*."

"Oh, I would love to see it."

They had a casual lunch, which Carolyn insisted was her treat. Jim ate with them but insisted that he pay for his meal.

Carolyn asked that Jim drive them by Kleinfeld's, which specialized in wedding dresses. "Adam will insist that you buy your wedding dress here. It is where my mother and I got our dresses. It is a family tradition to buy our wedding dresses there. I hope you won't mind if my mother and I help you pick it out. They have thousands of dresses to choose from."

"I haven't even thought about a wedding dress yet. Well, that is important that we come here right away once you come back for the holidays."

It was three o'clock when they headed back to Carolyn's house. Jim carried the Christmas presents that Angelina had bought for Adam and his family into Carolyn's house. "I promise to put them under my mom's tree. We always open gifts on Christmas Day. Angelina, I had a wonderful time shopping with you. Adam will be quizzing you about what you bought. He loves Christmas. He's just like a kid during the holidays."

Angelina and Carolyn hugged each other before Angelina got back in the car. "Carolyn, I am so glad that Adam has a sister. I always wanted a sister, but I was an only child. I already feel close to you."

Jim drove Angelina back to Cathy's estate. Angelina fell asleep during the ride. Jim opened the door for Adam to slip into the back seat of the car to wake Angelina up with a kiss. "Did you have a good shopping trip, darling?"

"Oh yes, it was wonderful. Carolyn is already like a sister to me. We finished all our Christmas shopping. I even got your Christmas present, Adam."

"Well, there are plenty of shopping days left till Christmas for you to get anything you may have forgotten." Adam winked at Angelina. "We will have to do some shopping together in December when we return. What is in the sack from Macy's?"

"It is something for me, but you can't see them until later tonight."

As they walked into the house, Angelina asked what he and his mom did all day.

"We mostly talked about you. She wanted to know all about you."

Angelina frowned. "Did you tell her about my stalker and my story?"

"Yes, I felt she needed to know. She is worried about you. She now understands why I am so protective of you and why I want to bring you back to New York to stay with me."

Chapter Twenty-Seven

Exploring New York City

When Angelina and Adam got back to Adam's apartment that night, Adam could tell she was tired. "I never did so much shopping, but I had a great time. I am going to change into something more comfortable, if you don't mind."

Angelina went into the bedroom and changed into one of her new nightgowns. When she came out, Adam's eyes got wide and turned dark.

"Do you like this, Adam? I bought it for you."

"You look good enough to eat. If you think you will be wearing this to bed, I'm afraid I will be having fun taking it off of you." He laughed.

Angelina next gasped. She ran to the balcony windows and said, "Look at the city lights! What a view of the city!"

"We'll get to enjoy it tonight and tomorrow night before we leave to go back to Cape Girardeau on Sunday."

"What do we have to do in Cape when we return?"

"Quite a bit. For one thing, we need to change your mailing address. I want to see Carl Johnson about any new developments in your stalker case. You also have a follow-up appointment with Alan Spindler. He wants to check on your head injury. I need to see a client. I also need to visit your old landlord to see if there are any loose ends with letting your apartment go. I want you to turn in your resignation at the hospital. That will give you a chance to say goodbye to your nursing friends and show off you engagement ring. If you want to invite any of them to our wedding, you can get their addresses. I'm sure we will think of other things."

"I think you have thought of everything."

Adam walked up behind Angelina and put his arms around her. She leaned her head back upon his chest. She felt her knees go weak. Adam picked her up and carried her to the sofa facing the windows so they could enjoy the city lights. Adam dimmed the lights. "I'm going to have a glass of wine. Do you want one?"

Angelina nodded yes. "Adam, do you think we will always continue to be this much in love? Do you think you will ever grow bored with me? I suppose that is my greatest fear."

"Darling, I promise to love you all the rest of my life. I have never felt this way about anyone and I can't imagine growing tired of you. We will grow old together, I promise."

Adam went to the phone and ordered some room service. "You will have to hide in the bedroom when the bellhop brings our snacks up. I don't want him to see you in your nightgown and get any ideas. I've already had enough trouble keeping other men from you. I see them staring at you all the time now."

After they had their snack, Adam took Angelina to the bedroom and took her to bed. Angelina thought he was right when he said she would be losing the nightgown. At least he didn't damage it when he took it off of her.

Angelina woke up the next morning snuggled in Adam's arms. She watched him while he slept. He was so handsome. She still had to pinch herself to make certain it was all not a dream. When he opened his eyes and saw she was looking at him, he smiled and said, "Good morning, darling. Did you sleep well?"

"I always sleep well when I am with you. You are so handsome. I never get tired of looking at you."

After they showered and got dressed, Adam again ordered room service for breakfast. "As usual, I am starving." He called Jim and invited him over to share breakfast with them and talk about the sights he wanted Angelina to see that day. It was a long itinerary that included all the tourist sites in New York. They decided to leave at ten o'clock. "Jim, I am hungry for Italian food, so choose an Italian restaurant and make reservations for tonight for Angelina and me for about 7:30 p.m."

"I'll do it, Adam."

Their day in New York was exciting. Adam showed her Wall Street and Old Trinity Church, which was the oldest church in the United States. They took the Staten Island Ferry over to the Statue of Liberty. They went up to the top of the Empire State Building to look out over the city. There was so much to see that Angelina was amazed.

They ate lunch and went back to the apartment about three o'clock. "I don't want to tire you out since we are going out tonight."

That night Adam took Angelina to an expensive Italian restaurant. He had her wear the sexy green dress he had bought her for the trip and her white mink coat. Adam wore a dark suit. Angelina was so proud to be on Adam's arm. The maître d' knew Adam. He showed them to their table. "Antonio, I want to introduce you to my fiancée, Angelina Harper. We are getting married in February."

Antonio immediately called for some pink champagne so they could toast their upcoming marriage. During their supper, a man and a woman came up to their table. Adam introduced them as one of his clients. Adam could tell the man was staring at Angelina. Adam pulled Angelina to his side as though to give the man the hint that she was his and to back off. "John, Angelina is my fiancée, and we are planning our marriage for February 29. I hope you can come."

"We'll plan on it, Adam," the man said as they excused themselves.

"I'm going to have to watch that guy," said Adam. "I don't like the way he looked at you."

"Oh, Adam, I am sure you are imagining things."

"Angelina, don't be naive. He looked like he wanted to molest you. It would be over my dead body before I would allow him to touch you."

When they got back to Adam's apartment, the answering machine was blinking with a call. Adam turned it on, and a man's voice said he would be calling back in an hour because he wanted to talk to "the whore."

Angelina's eyes filled with tears as Adam called to alert Jim to the obscene call. "You need to be particularly alert tonight because I don't know if the stalker has followed us here to New York. Alert the front desk to not allow the bellman to bring anyone up to the penthouse. I also don't want any more calls tonight."

Adam hung up and gathered Angelina into his arms. "Don't worry, darling. No one can get to us here. Please don't let this crazy man ruin our Thanksgiving holiday together."

Adam took a gun out of his bedside table and put it up on top of the table for easy access. Adam and Angelina went to bed as he wiped away Angelina's tears. "You will always be safe with me, darling."

Chapter Twenty-Eight

Back to Cape Girardeau

The trip back to Cape Girardeau was noneventful. Jim got their car out of the airport security lot and brought it around to pick them up and to load their luggage. When they got back to Adam's apartment, they unpacked, and Angelina started a load of laundry while Adam called Carl Johnson. Carl told him there were no new developments in finding their stalker. Adam told Carl about the obscene phone call they had received the night before coming home.

"I don't know how he found us in New York. I also don't know if he followed us to New York or just called us there."

"I will try and secure your phone records and find out."

"Thanks, Carl. Stay in touch."

Adam told Angelina he and Jim were going to check on her old apartment and to change her mailing address. "We will be back within the hour. Don't answer the phone or let anyone into the garage area." Adam bent down and gave her a kiss goodbye.

Adam and Jim were home just as he said they would be. Adam had retrieved Angelina's mail from the post office and handed it to her to sort through. "Your mail will be coming here from here on out."

As Angelina looked through her mail, she found a lot of advertisements along with a letter from John Noble. Angelina opened it to read. "Angelina, don't read that crazy man's rubbish," Adam said as he took the letter from her hands.

"Adam, I only read it to see what is on his mind. Don't you think we should at least do that?"

"I don't you to be upset or worry about this man any longer. Why don't you just let me read it and then take them to Carl Johnson. He needs to be kept informed."

"OK, darling," she said as she handed the letter to Adam. As she did so, a king of hearts playing card fell out of the letter. Angelina looked at it but did not become nervous or upset.

Adam read the letter and said it was filled with usual threats and declaration of his love. Adam put the letter in his pocket. "Tomorrow you have your appointment with Alan at one o'clock. I am anxious to hear how he thinks you are doing. You haven't had any headaches since we went to New York, have you?"

"No, I feel all cured."

"After your appointment, we will go to the hospital and turn in your resignation. I will also go with you to your nursing unit to announce our engagement to your fellow nursing comrades. Does that sound like a good plan?" asked Adam.

"Sounds good to me. I will hate to tell everyone goodbye though."

The next morning Angelina got dressed and Adam suggested they go out for lunch before her doctor's appointment. "Sounds good to me, Adam. Where shall we go?"

"How about Sunny Hill's Golden Coin?"

"I have only been there one other time. The hospital gave all the employees a gift certificate to the Golden Coin for Christmas about ten years ago. A fellow nurse and I went there for supper one night. It was very good food."

"The Golden Coin it is, then."

After lunch, Jim drove them to Angelina's appointment with Alan Spindler. Alan welcomed them back to Cape, asking how their New York trip had gone. Dr. Spindler examined Angelina and had a repeat CAT scan done. Afterwards he gave Angelina a clean bill of health. "You and Angelina will have to go out one night to celebrate your engagement while you are here. This is the first time that I ever played Cupid with any success." He smiled. "When is the wedding being planned for, Adam?"

"February 29. Since you are my Cupid, I would like for you to be my best man. Would you consider coming to New York for our wedding?"

"I accept, my good man."

Angelina left Alan's office for the hospital. When they arrived, they went straight to the personnel office to fill out the resignation forms. They next went to the nursing administrator's office to tell Angelina's boss. Angelina's boss marveled at Angelina's ring and congratulated Adam on catching Angelina.

"I am going over to the ICU if it is OK to say goodbye to everyone. I am really going to miss the nurses there."

"Well, Angelina, I want to wish you both the best of luck."

As they left for the ICU, Adam could tell that Angelina was getting a little sentimental about putting this nursing life behind her. "It will all be OK, darling. We are off on a brand new adventure."

All of the ICU staff gathered round Angelina as she showed them her engagement ring from Adam. They all carried on about the size of the diamond. Angelina told them that the wedding was being planned for February 29 and that all would be invited to come if they could get away and come to New York. She gave them each a hug and said goodbye. It was funny how time had changed everything.

Chapter Twenty-Nine

Return to New York

Adam saw some of his clients in Cape Girardeau before he and Angelina headed back to New York. Jim introduced Adam and Angelina to Tom Spencer once they got back to New York. "Tom is going to be my compadre. One of us will always be with you as usual while the other will take care of Angelina. I have known Tom for many years, and he is most trustworthy. He recently retired from the Secret Service and is looking for a job like this. His wife died about three years ago, and his children are all raised. He is all yours if you want him."

"I'm going to trust you, Jim, with this. Have you told him what we are up against?"

"He knows everything, Adam."

"In that case, welcome aboard, Tom. I am trusting you with our lives. I hope you know that. No one—and I mean no one—can come near Angelina without our approval. One of you must always be here with Angelina when I am away at work. If she wishes to go somewhere, you must take her and stay with her."

"Yes, sir, Mr. Harris. You have my word," said Tom.

"Jim will train you in the security system we have here, and when we travel to Cape, he will acclimate you to my apartment building layout there. I expect you to always have a gun and to monitor our apartments."

"Yes, sir. You can count on me."

Tom and Jim left, and the door securely shut behind them. Angelina was standing at the balcony windows. "I don't think I will ever grow tired of this view of New York City. Look, Adam, it is beginning to snow. It hasn't snowed since our first date together."

Adam came over to the windows and wrapped his arms around Angelina. "The snow is beautiful. I'll never forget our first date and how smitten I was with you." Adam went and turned on some soft music and starting dancing with Angelina. The song was "Only You."

"I think this should be our song, don't you, darling?"

"Yes, because you are my one and only love." Angelina stood on her tiptoes and kissed Adam. "Let's eat in tonight, watch old movies, watch it snow, and just snuggle. What do you think?"

"That's a grand idea. They are predicting about a foot of snow tonight. Who knows, we might get snowed in for days, and I wouldn't complain as long as I am with you. You can put on one of those hot little nightgown numbers that I can later take off you." Adam winked at Angelina.

"Oh, Adam, you are incorrigible."

"I'm being serious my love."

Adam ordered shrimp cocktail, salad, and steak for their supper along with a bottle of wine. When the bellhop rang, Adam ordered Angelina to the bedroom. After they ate, Adam found *Gone with the Wind* playing on TV.

"I love that movie, Adam. I always dreamed that I could write a book like that."

"Maybe someday you will. Don't sell yourself short," said Adam.

After the movie, Adam said, "I know why you like this movie. Scarlet has green eyes just like you, and Rhett Butler is a handsome dude."

"He is handsome and virile just like you."

"You think so, do you?" Adam went to the window and announced that there was a blizzard outside, and since there was nothing else they could do about it, he was taking her to bed.

Angelina giggled. Adam said, "So you think this is funny, do you? Well let me show you how funny this is."

Adam chased Angelina playfully around the apartment until he caught her. He picked her up and threw her over his shoulder and carried her to the bedroom. "I now have to tackle this nightgown, or I guess I could just tear it off of you."

"No, Adam, I want to keep it intact."

The phone then rang. Adam answered it. He said, "Listen, you jerk, I'm getting tired of your calling here in the middle of the night. I hope you roast in hell!" Adam slammed the receiver down and called the front desk. He told the clerk to not put through any more calls for the rest of the night and to not let anyone come up to the penthouse. He then called Jim and told him what had happened.

"That will take care of that nutcase for the night." Adam again put his gun on the nightstand, saying, "Angelina, do you know how to shoot a gun?"

"No, Adam, I don't. One time, my dad showed me how to shoot a shotgun. He always wanted me to go hunting with him, but guns scared me."

"Well, I am going to have Jim teach you."

Chapter Thirty

The Holidays with Adam

It was December 1, and one morning, Angelina asked Adam if they could get a Christmas tree for the apartment. "I always loved Christmas at home and the Christmas tree we had to celebrate the holidays. A Christmas tree would make me feel like Christmas when I turn on the lights at night."

"If that's what you want, sweetheart, I will have Jim purchase one."

"I had saved some of my old ornaments from home, but I think they were probably destroyed by the stalker when he ransacked my apartment."

"Well, you can go with Jim and pick out new ornaments to start the tradition of having our own tree together," said Adam.

"Oh, Adam, you spoil me so much. I love you," she said as she threw her arms around him and gave him a big kiss. "Have you talked with your mom or Carolyn since we got back in town?"

"Yes, I have. They want you to get together with them to start the wedding planning. Mom said that you and she need to put together a guest list and pick out wedding invitations. She has secured St. Patrick's Cathedral for February 29. That was the biggest thing of importance that had to be done first before you pick out invitations and have them printed.

Give her a call today and set up a time that you both can meet about all this."

"I'll do that, Adam. I hope you have a good day at work. What time will you be home, do you think?"

"Sometime after five." Adam gave Angelina a kiss goodbye, reminding Angelina to not leave the apartment anytime without Jim and to not open the door for anyone.

Angelina called Adam's mom about 10:00 a.m. Cathy Harris was so happy to hear from Angelina. "Can we get together tomorrow?" she asked. "I will come into the city and meet you at Adam's apartment. We will start putting together the guest list and then have Jim take us to the Waldorf to pick out the invitations and maybe even pick out your china and silver. Does that sound like fun? We can also set up an appointment when Carolyn and I can go with you to Kleinfeld's to pick out your wedding dress."

"A wedding dress? I hadn't thought about that."

"Well, we'll need to get that out of the way soon because of the need for possible alterations. That all takes time, my dear. You are going to make a beautiful bride. Adam will want you to have a beautiful dress for the occasion."

"This is a lot to take in, but it all sounds exciting. I'll see you at ten tomorrow."

Jim's voice came on over the apartment intercom. "May I come in, Ms. Angelina? I have something for you."

"Yes, Jim, you may."

Jim came in carrying a large cardboard box. "Adam said you are going to put up a Christmas tree, and I thought you may want this box."

Angelina opened the box and screamed with glee. "Jim, these are my Christmas decorations and ornaments from home. I thought they were lost or destroyed by the stalker. You found them and saved them for me. I may need you to take me out to purchase additional ornaments since our tree at home was never very big."

"I'd be happy to do that, ma'am. I will get a tree and set it up for you to decorate so you'll have some idea what you may need to buy. I know a place that has the best ornaments to choose from. You and Adam can start your own collection."

"Oh, Jim, You are wonderful. Thanks you for all you do for us."

Later that day, Jim came in with a big Christmas tree with the help of the bellman. They set the tree up in the stand. It was about eight feet tall and beautifully shaped.

"It is an artificial tree. I hope you don't mind. The hotel doesn't allow real trees because of the fire hazard. Besides, you can leave it up as long as you wish after Christmas."

"At home we always left ours up until after New Year's Day. It is perfect, Jim. Can we go and pick out ornaments now?"

"Certainly, we can. The store is not that far away."

Jim took Angelina out shopping. Angelina was so excited to get out of the hotel for a little while. She had a great time at the Christmas decorations store. When she was finished picking out the ornaments and decorations, she told Jim she hoped that Adam wouldn't be angry that she spent so much.

"He loves you, Ms. Angelina. He wants to buy you the moon."

Chapter Thirty-One

Wedding Planning

When Adam came home from work, he found Angelina standing on a chair on her tiptoes, stringing Christmas lights on their new tree. He lifted her down from the chair, saying, "What the hell do you think you are doing, baby?"

"Adam, look at the Christmas tree that Jim got for us. He set it up and everything. He took me to the Christmas shop not too far from here and let me pick out all the lights and decorations. He even brought me a box of Christmas decorations that I had saved from home. I didn't even know that he had them. I am so excited that I decided to get started before you came home. I want to finish decorating it tonight so that we can start enjoying it at night."

"That is great, darling, but I don't want you up on a chair on your tiptoes. You could fall and hurt yourself. Let Jim or me do the tall decorating."

"I want you and not Jim. It is our first tree together."

"OK, darling. Let me do the stuff up high though." Adam kissed Angelina as he put her down. "Tell me about the rest of your day. Did you talk to my mom?"

"I did. She is coming here to the apartment at ten so that we can start the wedding planning. We are going to work on a guest list and have Jim take us to the Waldorf to pick out wedding invitations. She says I need to pick out china, crystal, and silver while we are there. I kind of want your approval before that is put in stone."

"Darling, you don't need my approval. I will love whatever you pick out. My mom has good taste too."

Jim called Adam on the intercom and asked him to come to his apartment for a minute. When Adam went in to see Jim, he saw this huge bouquet of funeral flowers that included gladiolas and other funerary flowers.

"Don't tell me. These are from Angelina's stalker. What florist did they come from? Maybe you can get a lead on this madman from them. Get rid of these flowers, and don't tell Angelina about them."

"I'll do it now, boss. Do you think this guy is in New York?"

"I don't know, but I am going to let Carl Johnson know in Cape about this development. Angelina is having so much fun with our new Christmas tree I don't want to ruin it for her. You be extra vigilant tomorrow when you take my mom and Angelina to the Waldorf. Close the floor and my phone down for the night please."

Adam and Angelina finished their Christmas tree after supper and sat on the couch, admiring it with the lights in the apartment turned down low.

"Isn't it beautiful, Adam? The pink angel ornament is as old as I am. It was mine at home, and my parents got it for me when I was born. It was made in Germany. I am so happy that Jim salvaged my box of decorations from home. They make Christmas special."

Angelina fell asleep with her head on Adam's shoulder, and he carried he to bed. He snuggled her in his arms and thanked God for bringing her into his life. The next morning, once Adam went to work, Angelina dressed for her meeting with Cathy Harris at ten o'clock.

They put a preliminary guest together before going out for lunch. Jim then took them to the Waldorf to see the wedding planners there to look at invitations. Angelina picked an invitation that had a castle and a horse-drawn carriage taking the wedding company up the path to the castle. The card read on the front "Dreams do come true."

"I love that invitation also, Angelina. Let's give them the inside details for the invitation and place the order. Now let's go look at china, crystal, and silverware."

"The china is all so elegant." Angelina finally settled on a Lenox pattern with silver trim. She also picked out matching crystal and silverware that was absolutely perfect. "Do you think Adam will like it, Mrs. Harris?

"I am positive he will. You have good taste, Angelina."

On the ride back to the hotel, Angelina made a date to go shopping for her wedding gown with Adam's mom and his sister Carolyn for next Tuesday. "It is a tradition for our family to all buy our gowns at Kleinfeld's. If you can't find the perfect dress there, you won't be able to find one."

"I can't believe I am going to be picking out a wedding dress. I have always believed that I would never get married. Then I met Adam. It is like I am living a dream."

"I have never seen my son so happy, Angelina. You two are perfect for each other."

"I can't believe that he has been single all these years. I'm sure there have been a lot of women after him."

"There have been many who thought they could nab him, but they were all too obvious, and he didn't like being chased after. He told me about you right away and said he felt that he couldn't live without you. He said he loved you from the first moment he saw you. I'm happy he found you, Angelina."

"I only hope that I can keep him happy forever."

Chapter Thirty-Two

The King of Hearts Escapes

Adam came early from work that day. He first went to see Jim and Tom. "I need to tell you that I had a call from the Cape Girardeau police department telling me that John Noble, the original King of Hearts, has escaped from the Missouri State Prison in Jefferson City. They seem to think that he is headed this way. I am worried about Angelina, of course. I want the two of you to pass his photo around with the hotel staff even though I feel he will be caught before he ever makes it here. I am going to tell Angelina tonight, and I don't want the two of you to leave her alone here. Jim, I want you to teach her to handle and fire handguns accurately because I have been letting mine sit out on the nightstand every night."

"Yes, sir, we understand. You can count on us, sir."

Adam went into the apartment and found Angelina napping on the couch. She looked so fragile there. He sat on a chair near to her and just watched he sleep. He thought about how much he loved her. He had this worried look on his face when she woke up.

"Adam, you're home." Angelina jumped up and went and sat on Adam's lap. "Why are you home so early?"

"I have something to tell you," he said. "I had a call from Carl Johnson in Cape Girardeau. He told me that John Noble has escaped from prison and the state police think he is headed this way. I have talked to Jim and Tom and given them important instructions. I don't want you get too worried about this. You are well protected here. I have asked Jim and Tom to not let you out of their sight. Until this guy is recaptured, I want you to stay here in the apartment."

Angelina started trembling and crying. "I knew you would get upset about this. Remember what I told you when we first started dating? I told you I would protect and take care of you forever. That is just what I am doing." Adam cradled Angelina in his arms and kissed her. He kissed away her tears and said, "I pity any man who attempts to get to you. I have brought you a present." He went to the intercom and told Jim to bring in Angelina's gift. "It's something to keep you company when I am at work."

Just then Jim opened the apartment and ushered in a big German shepherd dog. "His name is Sam. He is trained in defense. The boys will see that he is taken care of and fed. Your job is to make friends with Sam so he knows you are his main job."

"Oh, Adam, he is beautiful. I already love him." Sam wagged his tail and licked Angelina's face.

"I believe the police will recapture John Noble soon. It is a long way between here and Jefferson City, Missouri. He doesn't know where we are exactly, does he, Adam?"

Adam shook his head no even though it was probably a lie. Adam knew her stalker that reported everything to John Noble and he knew where they lived. He had had the funeral flowers delivered to the apartment.

"Darling, why don't we all go downstairs to the restaurant here at the hotel and have supper?"

"That sounds great. I'll get dressed. Sam, are you coming with me? If you don't, I know Adam will."

"Angelina, if you think I am going to let Sam replace my opportunities to watch you dress, you are mistaken," Adam said laughingly as he chased her into the bedroom.

When Angelina and Adam went downstairs to the restaurant, Jim and Tom came along and ate with them. Angelina asked Jim and Tom about their lives in the Secret Service. "I think that must have been an exciting job during the sixties when the Kennedy brothers were killed. Were the two of you assigned to them?"

"No, we both had different assignments, such as Tom was assigned to Vice President Johnson and I was assigned to Jackie Kennedy and the children."

"Were you there in Texas when President Kennedy was killed in that motorcade?"

"I'm sorry to say I was. It was an awful day that I will never forget. I stayed with Jackie Kennedy while they took her husband into the ER. She was in a state of shock. When they came out and told her that the President was dead, I had to catch her before she collapsed on the floor. There was no one there but me to console her. I couldn't wait to get her out of there. News media were everywhere. It was chaos."

Tom said, "Then in the blink of an eye, I was assigned to protecting Vice President Johnson, soon to be sworn in as president on the plane as we headed back to Washington DC. That entire week after the assassination became a blur to me."

While they were talking, Adam noticed a man eating by himself in the restaurant. He seemed to be watching Angelina, and Adam didn't like it. He leaned over to Jim and said something to him that Angelina couldn't hear. Jim and Adam got up and went over to the man's table. "I noticed you have been staring at my fiancée. Is there a reason for your rudeness, sir?"

"I first was struck by her beauty, and then I noticed the big diamond on her finger. I'm sorry for being so rude. I am the hotel security officer, Don Jones. I guess I am paid to notice expensive jewelry like that on hotel guests. What room are you staying in?"

"I'm afraid that is none of your business," said Jim. "Excuse us."

"I want you check on him after supper to make sure that Don Jones is who he says he is, Jim."

They went back to their table with Angelina and Tom. The stranger got up and left. After supper they all went back to the penthouse while Jim stayed at the front desk to check on Don Jones for Adam. Adam and Angelina relaxed on the couch, with the Christmas tree lights glowing and some soft music playing. Jim knocked on the door, and Adam went to talk with Jim. Jim let Sam the dog in, and Sam went immediately to Angelina, wagging his tail.

"Don Jones is not employed by the hotel, Adam. Hotel management has copied his picture from the security cameras and are going to be watching for him. Do you think he could be Ms. Angelina's stalker? If it was John Noble, Angelina would have recognized him. Do you want to keep Sam in the apartment tonight?"

"Yes, leave Sam. He might as well get used to the place. You and Tom keep that man's picture in mind because we might be seeing him again."

About two days later, Adam got another call from Carl Johnson in Cape Girardeau. This time he learned that John Noble had been recaptured near Philadelphia. "I certainly am glad they caught him, Carl. Thanks for letting me know. Angelina has been scared and depressed, and this will cheer her up."

Chapter Thirty-Three

Christmas and New Year's

Angelina and Cathy Harris worked on the wedding plans through the day while Adam was at work. At night Angelina and Adam were busy going to holiday parties and going out shopping for Christmas and enjoying the spirit of Christmas in the city. Cathy Harris and her daughter, Carolyn, took Angelina to Kleinfeld's to shop for a wedding dress. The wedding planner at Kleinfeld's told them that since it was less than nine months till the wedding, they would not have time to order her the dress of her choosing. "I will have to get special permission to sell you a dress off the racks. Luckily your size will lend itself well to doing that. Let's get started. What is your budget for the dress?" she asked.

Mrs. Harris said, "There is no budget. If we love it, we'll buy it."

The clerk put Angelina into several different gowns, but Carolyn and Cathy didn't seem to like any of them. Angelina thought they all were beautiful. Cathy Harris said that this was to be a special dress since her son and Angelina were getting married at St. Patrick's Cathedral.

The next dress that Angelina tried on was so beautiful that Angelina began to cry. "That's the dress!" said Cathy and Carolyn. "Now let's see a long veil and a tiara."

"Angelina, you make the most beautiful bride."

"What do you mean, Mom? She is drop-dead gorgeous," said Carolyn.

They picked out shoes and jewelry. By the time it was over, Angelina was exhausted. "Let's go for lunch."

Tom and Jim ate at a different table so that the three women could continue talking about wedding plans. Once lunch was over, they started to leave when a young woman came to Cathy and said, "Aren't you Adam Harris's mother? How is Adam anyway? He hasn't called me for a date in months."

"Adam is fine. Let me introduce you to Adam's fiancée. Angelina, this is Sarah Rice. Sarah, this is Angelina Harper. They are getting married the end of February."

The woman said congratulations and then excused herself, saying, "Tell Adam hello for me."

As she left, Cathy Harris said, "Over our dead bodies."

When Angelina got home, she collapsed on the couch from exhaustion. One of Adam's old girlfriends had to ruin a perfectly great day. Angelina wondered what Adam saw in her and how long they had dated. She wondered if he had had sex with her.

When Adam came home, Angelina told him that Sarah Rice had told her to say hello. Adam stared at Angelina and asked what else she had said. "She said you hadn't called her for a date in a long time. How long had you dated her, Adam?"

"I dated her about two months is all. Angelina, I can tell she upset you. She meant nothing to me, darling. You're the one wearing my ring.

You are going to be my wife. How could you let any woman affect you this way? You are so much more beautiful than her. Tell me about the rest of your day."

Adam picked Angelina up and carried her to a chair so she could sit on his lap.

"Well, I picked out my wedding dress. Your mom and Carolyn said you will love it."

"I can hardly wait until you are mine. You would look good in a potato sack."

Christmas Eve, Angelina and Adam went to Carolyn's house with gifts and to watch their girls open their gifts. It was great fun to get to know their girls and Carolyn's husband better. The next day was Christmas at Adam's mom's house. They had a formal lunch and then spent the evening opening gifts. Adam's nieces handed out the presents one by one to open. When it came time for Adam to open Angelina's gift to him, he shook it and smiled. "What is it, Angelina?" When he opened it, he was surprised.

"Do you like it, Adam? Maurice said you had nothing like it, so I couldn't resist."

"I love it, darling. I will never take it off."

"I had it engraved inside." Adam read the engraving that said, "With all my love, Angelina."

A little while later, Adam took a small package out of his pocket and gave it to Angelina. Angelina was nervous and excited as she opened Adam's gift. Her eyes grew wide as she opened the box. It too was bought at Maurice's. It was an emerald tennis bracelet with a matching set of earrings and necklace.

"Oh, Adam, it is beautiful. I love it."

Everyone gathered around Angelina to look at her gift from Adam. They knew he was going to get her something very special. "You will have to wear it for me on New Year's Eve with your green dress."

New Year's Eve came, and Adam took Angelina to a party at the country club. There was a band, and she met a lot of new people who were Adam's friends. They all seemed really nice. Adam and Angelina danced the night away in each other's arms until the band starting playing "Auld Lang Syne." Adam bent down and gave Angelina a New Year's kiss and said, "I love you, Angelina. This our first New Year's kiss. There will be many more when we get home."

Angelina smiled up at Adam and said, "Um, that sounds promising."

"I'll go get your wrap so we can head home. I can't wait to take you to bed."

Angelina felt like a teenager because Adam didn't stop kissing her until they arrived at the hotel. When they arrived at their apartment, Adam picked Angelina up, carried her to the bedroom, and made love to her. "I want this to be a New Year's that you never forget, Angelina. I know I won't."

After their passion was spent, Angelina and Adam snuggled together in his big bed and fell asleep shortly thereafter.

Chapter Thirty-Four

More Fun and Games

It was the middle of January, and it was about six weeks until Angelina and Adam's wedding. Angelina had asked Carolyn to be her maid of honor and had asked the little girls to serve as flower girls. Adam's best man was going to be Carolyn's husband. Everything was falling into place.

One day, Angelina asked who she might have give her away at the wedding since her father wasn't living. "I thought I might ask Alan Spindler, since he was our Cupid on the day we met. What do you think?"

"I think that is a great idea. Give him a call. I know he will do it."

Family friends were hosting bridal showers for Angelina. Cathy hosted a lingerie shower for Angelina. The things she got were all beautiful. She hid them away from Adam's sight. One of Adam's aunts gave her a household shower. They got so many really nice things. Angelina spent many days sending out thank-you cards. One day it struck Angelina that she had not bought Adam's wedding ring yet. She called Jim in and asked him to take her to Maurice's so she could pick out Adam's ring.

Maurice was so helpful. He showed her a ring that went perfectly with her engagement ring. "I love it, but I don't know Adam's ring size."

"I will find out, Ms. Angelina. I will have it delivered when it is sized and ready."

When they got back to the apartment. Tom met Angelina with a package from Cape Girardeau. It was from the hospital staff she worked with in the ICU. Angelina began to open it when she heard a ticking noise. She panicked and screamed out for Jim. The package exploded, knocking Angelina to the ground. Tom and Jim came running in and immediately called the police and an ambulance. They also called Adam. Angelina was coughing, but she said she was all right. "It was like a smoke bomb. It was loud though." The room was filled with smoke, so Jim opened the balcony door. The police arrived along with the paramedics. Adam arrived a short time later.

Angelina's face was black with the soot from the bomb. Adam scooped Angelina up in his arms and asked Jim and Tom what happened. "It's not their fault, Adam. We thought it was a wedding gift from the nurses at Cape Girardeau. It just went off when I opened it."

"Well, that tells me you are not to open any more packages for now. You got that, boys?"

"Mr. Harris, I think we need to take her to the hospital and have her checked out."

"Yes, I will go with her. Jim, I'll meet you at the hospital."

The police said the smoke bomb was meant as a warning. "If they had wanted to really kill her, they could have done so."

Angelina was released the next morning.

Adam called and told Carl Johnson about the attack. "We looked at the hotel video footage and discovered that the man who delivered the package was a man by the name of Don Jones, which is most likely an alias. I met him in the hotel restaurant when I caught him staring at Angelina. He claimed he was the hotel security guard, which I found out later was not true. Carl, I am going to fax you a picture of this man. Maybe you will recognize him. I believe this is Angelina's stalker and keeps in contact with John Noble. I think we are getting closer to solving this mystery."

"I'll let you know if I find anything on this end, Adam. In the meantime, you two stay safe."

Adam talked to Tom and Jim the next morning. "Don't let Angelina open any more packages. Keep them until you have enough to take to the hospital to have them x-rayed. Once we know they are safe, then Angelina and I can open them."

The wedding day finally came, and Adam couldn't wait to make Angelina his bride. It was a beautiful February day. The sun was shining even though it was cold. Other than threatening phone calls, things seemed to be slowing down with the stalker. Only Adam's mom knew where they were going to honeymoon. They were going to spend a week in Paris. Alan Spindler escorted Angelina down the aisle. Adam's eyes grew brilliant when he saw Angelina coming toward him. When she arrived beside her, he whispered she looked beautiful. The ceremony went so fast. They exchanged vows and rings, and that was that. All that preparation culminating in marriage. Angelina smiled up at Adam as he bent down to kiss her once the priest said, "I now pronounce you man and wife."

The bells at St. Patrick's started ringing as Adam and Angelina stood in a receiving line at the back of the church, greeting guests. Jim was driving the limo and helped Angelina and Adam into the car, and they left for more picture-taking and the reception. "I can't believe we are married. Adam, I love you so much. I am so lucky to have you as my husband."

"No, I am the lucky one, darling. You've made an honest man of me. I was beginning to think I would never find a woman like you. I am blessed. Now we get to dance the night away and leave on our honeymoon."

"Adam, you haven't told me where we are going."

"Paris for a week, my love. It's the City of Romance, you know."

"When do we leave?"

"Our plane leaves at 1:00 a.m. We'll be able to sleep during the flight. What are you frowning about? Oh, I know you are wondering when we can consummate our marriage. I thought and planned for that. We will leave the reception about 9:00 p.m. and go to the hotel to dress for the trip. I plan to make passionate love to you and make an honest woman of you before we travel," Adam said as he gave her a loving kiss.

Chapter Thirty-Five

Mr. and Mrs. Adam Harris

Angelina and Adam returned from their honeymoon and settled into the apartment as the newlyweds. The hotel staff seemed to smile every time they saw the couple together, as though they never saw them before. Even Jim and Tom were happy that they were finally married. They all seemed to notice a change in Angelina. She was smiling all the time and was truly happy. Adam was the perfect husband and lover. She could hardly wait for him to come home from work because she knew he would be hers for the night. During the day Angelina busied herself with the writing of thank-you cards to all the friends and family who had given them wedding gifts. Adam and Angelina had decided to store most of the gifts at his mom's estate until they were ready to buy a home.

After the couple had been married about six weeks, Adam came home and found Angelina passed out on the living room floor. Adam ran to her side and called Jim and Tom into the apartment. "Jim, call an ambulance quickly. I don't know what has happened to Angelina. Did she seem well today?"

"She has been fine. I brought Sam in to her after his morning walk, and she was sitting on the sofa reading a book. This afternoon we took her to the gun range to start teaching Angelina how to fire a gun."

Angelina started to stir. "What happened to you, darling?" As Angelina's eyes came into focus she saw Adam's worried face and reached up to touch him. "I don't know. I stood up to see what the sirens were all about on the street, and I just passed out, I guess."

Adam asked if she had any pain anywhere, and once she said no, he picked her up and laid her on the sofa. "We called an ambulance, and they will be here any minute. We are going to have this checked out."

Angelina was admitted to the hospital ER, and they began running tests on her. "I feel so foolish," she told the ER physician. "I feel fine right now."

"Well, we'll get to the bottom of this. We've drawn blood work and done several other tests. We should know something soon."

About one hour later, the doctor came back into Angelina's room. "Well, we now know what has happened to you, Mrs. Harris. You are pregnant. I hope the two of you find this as good news."

Angelina's mouth fell open. Adam jumped up and went to Angelina's side and took her hand. "Well, this is the best news a man like me could get." Adam kissed Angelina's hand.

Angelina said, "Adam, you told me you didn't think we could have children."

"The doctor's told me when I was a child and had surgery for undescended testicles that I could end up sterile. I guess they were wrong."

"I am going to let you go home, young lady, and let the two of you adjust to this news together," said the doctor. "You just need to take it easy for now. Mr. Harris, you said that she has been learning to fire a gun. I think it would be a good idea if Angelina dropped that project for now."

When Adam and Angelina got to the car, Adam told Jim that he and Tom now had three people to look after. Jim got this puzzled look on his face then realized what Adam had said, "Oh my god. Congratulations!."

"By the way, she can do no more firing of a gun for now."

"Adam, we need to tell your mom this weekend," said Angelina.

That evening Adam and Angelina went to the hotel restaurant to celebrate their news. Adam ordered them both a glass of champagne. He lifted his glass and said, "To our little baby that we made together on our honeymoon and had a lot of fun doing it."

"Adam, I hope you are happy with this news. I maybe should have gone on the pill for a while. I just never dreamed this could happen."

"Over my dead body were you going on the pill. I want his baby. Aren't you happy, Angelina?"

"I am elated. I dreamed about having your children, and now that dream is coming true."

Adam and Angelina talked about their future with a baby and started to talk about names. "Will you still love me when my belly starts getting big, Adam?"

"You know I will always love you, and I will prove it again tonight when I take you to my bed."

Chapter Thirty-Six

The Endgame

Angelina's pregnancy was going well. She was now six months along. Adam was seeing after her every need. He called her from work several times a day. The doctor told Angelina she was not gaining much weight, but he wasn't too worried. He had her on prenatal vitamins. He ordered an ultrasound to check on the baby and said the baby was fine. He asked Adam and Angelina if they wanted to know the baby's sex. They both decided to wait and be surprised.

The doctor told Adam and Angelina that he didn't want Angelina traveling until after the baby was born. "That means you won't be able to fly with me to Cape Girardeau for now?"

"Oh, Adam, we have never been separated since our marriage. I am going to miss you when you're gone to Cape."

"I won't go any more than I have to. Jim and Sam will always see after you."

Angelina settled into the idea of spending some lonely nights without Adam. She didn't know that Jim and Tom were intercepting the letters that John Noble had been sending her. Adam always read them just to see how radical he was getting and what was on his mind. They were always threatening letters, and he would always include a king of hearts playing card and would sign the letters "Love, the King of Hearts."

Adam told Jim and Tom that the nutcase was still obsessed with Angelina and that they should not let their vigilance down. "I'm certain from the content of these letters that the stalker is reporting everything to the King of Hearts. He knows Angelina is pregnant and threatens to harm her and our baby. Please, please don't let her out of your sight. I am going to Cape Girardeau on Friday and won't be back until Monday. I am going to worry myself silly. I am going to leave both of you here with Angelina this time. I can manage on my own."

That night Adam held Angelina close and told her he couldn't live without her. He had his hand on her little belly, and his eyes got wide when he felt the baby kick for the first time. He kissed her belly and kissed her mouth ever so tenderly. "Don't ever forget that I love you, Angelina."

Adam left early the next morning. Angelina asked Jim to take her to the library to get a couple of books she could read while Adam was gone. She liked murder mysteries. It didn't take her long to pick them out. As they were walking out of the library, a man rushed by Angelina, almost pushing her to the ground. If Jim hadn't been beside her, she would have fallen. The man ran off as Jim yelled at him to stop. Jim realized that it was Angelina's stalker.

Jim later told Tom about the incident, and when he talked to Adam that night, he told Adam. "Damn!" said Adam. "I wish I had been there. We could have caught him."

"I didn't want to chase him and leave Angelina alone."

"You did the right thing, Jim."

It rained all day Saturday, so Angelina stayed in the apartment, reading.

It was a gloomy day, and Angelina really missed Adam. She decided to take an early supper and watch old movies on TV. Jim came to take Sam out for his evening constitutional. Tom stayed behind to monitor the apartment and to be close in case Angelina needed something.

Suddenly Angelina heard some loud voices in the hallway, followed by some type of fighting. She ran to the door and looked out the peephole but didn't see but one man. It was the man that Adam had words with one night in the restaurant a few months ago for staring at Angelina. She realized that it was the same man who had almost knocked her down at the library. Was he the stalker?

Angelina panicked and ran to the bedroom where Adam had his gun sitting on the nightstand. She took the gun and went to hide in the closet. She wondered where Tom was and hoped Jim would be back soon with Sam. Angelina suddenly felt all alone. She stayed very quiet and listened for any noise. She then heard a strange voice say, "Angelina, where are you?" Angelina started trembling and realized she was all alone. She sat on the floor in the closet, holding the gun in her hands, pointing it at the closet door so she could shoot if need be. She made sure the safety was turned off just as Jim had taught her.

"Angelina," the voice said again, "you can run, but you can't hide for long. I'm going to find you, and then you know what? I'm going to kill you for my stepbrother, John Noble. He says it's time for you to die."

Tears came to Angelina's eyes. She thought about Adam and their baby. If she died, Adam's baby would die also. She thought to herself that she couldn't let that happen. She took a deep breath to steady her hands on the gun. She could hear footsteps getting closer. When the closet door opened, there stood a man in dark clothing holding a big knife. Without thinking, she started pulling the trigger to the gun until all the bullets were spent. The man fell backward and collapsed on the bedroom floor.

Angelina struggled to stand up and started to run out of the bedroom, but the man's hand grabbed her ankle to pull her down. As she struggled to get away, she heard Sam growl, and he attacked the man's hand. Jim came running into the bedroom with his gun raised but then stopped and called Sam off. The stalker was dead, and Angelina had killed him. Angelina started to faint. Jim caught her and carried her to the couch.

Jim called 911 and called the front desk to send some help. Angelina heard him say that Tom had been killed and their elevator man had been stabbed. He hung up and went to get Angelina's fuzzy robe and helped her on with it. He knew Adam would not let anyone to see her in a fancy negligee. Those nightgowns were for Adam's eyes only. Angelina was trembling and crying. When Angelina started to sit down, she grabbed her belly in pain. Jim called 911 again for an ambulance to take Angelina to the hospital. He hoped Angelina wasn't going to have a miscarriage. He next called Adam.

"Boss," he said, "there has been an incident here, and you need to come home now." Jim told Adam what had happened and that Angelina was on her way to the hospital. He also told Adam that Tom was killed trying to stop the stalker from entering the apartment. He laid it all out for Adam. "Angelina remembered the one gun lesson I gave her, and she shot that sucker dead. What a woman you have, Adam."

"I'll be home in a few hours, Jim. And say, Jim, thank you for being there."

Adam went straight to the hospital when he arrived in New York. He pulled up a chair beside Angelina's bed and began to cry. He prayed that God would not take their baby. He thanked God for sparing Angelina's life. He laid his head down on the bed, and he held on to Angelina's hand. He fell asleep there. He woke up to feeling a soft hand stoking his forehead. "Adam," she whispered. "I love you. I'm afraid I made a mess of things. Do you know if the baby is OK?"

"I haven't seen the doctor yet, honey. How are you feeling? I've been so worried about you. The plane seemed to take forever to get here."

"I think I am doing all right. I don't feel any labor pains right now, but I don't know what that means. The last time I shot a gun, I went into premature labor, remember."

"Yes, and the doctor told you not shoot a gun again while you were pregnant."

"I had to, Adam, or that guy was going to stab me to death. All I could think about was you and our little baby. I am so glad that Jim taught me what he did about handling a gun." Angelina got a sad look on her face. "Jim told me that the stalker killed Tom as he was trying to stop him from going into our apartment. That stalker was such an evil man."

"He's gone from our lives forever, Angelina. The police told me that he was John Noble's stepbrother. That's how John Noble knew what was going on in our lives."

The doctor came in a little later and told Adam and Angelina that the baby appeared fine. "We stopped your early labor, but I'm afraid you going to have to stay here a few days for observation."

"We can do that, Doctor, now that the stalker is out of our lives forever. This is a great day. It couldn't get any better than this."

"Well, I guess I can tell you both now that you are getting a twofer."

Adam asked the doctor, "What does that mean, Doc?"

"Why, you're having twins, my boy—twins!"

Chapter Thirty-Seven

The Final Journey

We never know ahead of time what life has in store for us. We can try and control our lives, but things often don't go as they are planned. Angeline lived fifteen of her years in constant fear and uncertainty. She never thought she was going to marry, much less have children. She never thought she could be a good mother after all she had been through. She met the man of her dreams, and everything fell into place. Adam and Angelina had their twins, a boy named Antonio and a girl named Angela.

Adam died at the ripe old age of eighty-five, and Angelina followed shortly thereafter at the age of eighty-two. They loved each other right up until the end. Angelina granted only one interview with a newspaper columnist during the last day of her life. She told her story. As she talked to the reporter, he asked her about her beautiful diamond ring.

"That was the engagement ring that Adam bought when he asked me to marry him. I have never taken it off. The two emeralds, Adam said, were for my green eyes. I'll never forget the night he gave me this ring. I was on cloud nine the rest of life with him. I miss him so much. Other than my children and grandchildren, I don't have much left to live for. I thought my mother was strange when she told me she didn't want to live anymore after my dad died. I now understand her and feel the same way. I think I am dying of a broken heart too."

The news reporter asked Angelina about her house that she had lived with Adam in for the last twenty-five years. She said she always loved this house as a little girl. She was raised in a modest home about four blocks away. "Every time I walked or drove by it, I was fascinated as a child. I would walk by it and imagine that I lived there. Once when I was a little girl, I made my mom and dad drive me to this house on Halloween to trick or treat. I thought because these people were rich, they had to have the best candy. I really just wanted to see into the house. You know, this house has always been called the boat house because it is in the shape of a boat. The man who had it built was a riverboat builder on the Mississippi River. He once went to prison for forging a check. When he got out, he bought this property to build his house on. The rich neighbors around this block didn't want him to build here because they thought he was going to build a shack. Well, as you can tell he built the best house in town. Adam knew I always loved this house, and he bought it for me for my birthday one year. He let me renovate it the way I wanted it. I love this house."

"Ms. Angelina, would you tell me the story of John Noble and his stepbrother and how they affected your life? I guess you know that John Noble died in prison this week?"

"Yes, I have heard. I am happy he is gone. I just wish he had died sooner. He made me reclusive for the better part of my life. I was afraid. He never gave up on me. Toward the end he had wanted to kill me and almost succeeded. His stepbrother became a stalker for him so he could keep me afraid and alone. If Adam had not come along when he did, I think I never would have married or had children. Adam had enough money to hire bodyguards for me. As long as Adam was with me, I wasn't afraid."

The newsman asked a lot of other questions about Angelina's life, and when he was done, he asked if she had any other thoughts to share?

"Most everyone in Cape Girardeau knows me and my story. I hope that when I am gone, I will be remembered kindly. I hope that they also remember the seven young men that the King of Hearts killed when I was a teenager. They deserved to have long and happy lives also. If it hadn't been for my husband, Adam, I don't think I would have lived these eighty-two years. I would have been a pitiful, sad woman."

That night, Angelina Harris Harper died. When they found her, she had a smile on her face. She was now with her Adam.

About The Author

Gwen Beaudean Thoma, EdD, was born and raised in Cape Girardeau, Missouri, a small college town along the Mississippi River. She attended the local college and graduated in 1969 with her basic nursing degree. Gwen was a registered professional nurse for forty-two years at Southeast Missouri Hospital. During that time, she continued her education, receiving her bachelor's degree in nursing and a master's degree in administration at Southeast Missouri State University. In 1999 Gwen graduated from the University of Memphis with her doctorate in education. Dr. Thoma loves to write and published her first book in 2016 entitled *No More Biting*. It is a children's book written for parents, grandparents, and teachers who have children who bite. It was written originally for her grandson in 2001. He had trouble with biting his friends at school. After retiring in 2011, Dr. Thoma decided to have it published. She wrote one other children's book, *The Cat Named Bud*, before moving into serious fiction.

Events in Dr. Thoma's life entangled her in five murders in Cape Girardeau. These murders changed her life forever and followed her for thirty years. Thus in 2015, Gwen wrote this book entitled *Living with Murder for Thirty Years*. Her love for writing is like a second career, and even though the differences between children's books and murder mysteries are huge, Dr. Thoma believes one should never limit possibilities in writing and authorship. Dr. Thoma also has written two other murder mysteries, *Whatever Happened to Sara?* and *The King of Hearts*. Now she has completed her sixth book, which is the sequel to *The King of Hearts*.

Lightning Source UK Ltd.
Milton Keynes UK
UKHW010631100820
367987UK00001B/159